D1013212

We want to hear from you. Please send your comments about this book to us in care of zreview@zondervan.com. Thank you.

Wild Horse Spring

Copyright © 2012 by Lisa Williams Kline

This title is also available as a Zondervan ebook.

Visit www.zondervan.com/ebooks

Requests for information should be addressed to:

Zonderkidz, 5300 Patterson Ave. SE, Grand Rapids, Michigan 49530

ISBN: 978-0-310-72615-9

Cover design: *Kris Nelson*
Interior design: *Ben Fetterly*
Editor: *Kim Childress*

Printed in the United States of America

12 13 14 15 16 17 18 19 20 /DCI/ 18 17 16 15 14 13 12 11 10 9 8 7 6 5 4 3 2 1

SISTERS IN ALL SEASONS

WILD HORSE
SPRING

SISTERS IN ALL SEASONS

BOOK TWO

WILD HORSE SPRING

By LISA WILLIAMS KLINE

ZONDERkidz

ZONDERVAN.com/
AUTHORTRACKER
follow your favorite authors

To my husband, Jeff

1

DIANA

"There's the third bridge!" Stephanie sat up and looked eagerly out the car window. "When you make it to the third bridge, you know you're almost there," she told me, poking my arm. "Look, Diana! See the water?"

I hated it when Stephanie knew more about something than I did. We were packed in the car on our way to spend spring break at North Carolina's Outer Banks. Stephanie had vacationed there with her dad for several years, but it was a first for me and Mom. And a first for all of us together. Our new family. Stephanie would probably spend the whole week telling me stuff I didn't know. Would I ever stop being jealous of her clear, tanned skin, and her wavy, dark hair? Her perfectly polished toenails?

As our car passed onto the bridge, I craned my neck, watching the choppy, sun-splashed, blue-green waves beyond the bridge rail. A seagull glided a few yards above, as if racing us, then banked and angled away. We passed a cluster of small flat islands with marshy vegetation and seabirds scavenging on the sandy shore.

Norm rolled down the driver's window, and we were buffeted by humid, salty sea air. "Just smell that!" He smiled over at my mom and grasped her hand. "I love this place, Lynn. I can't wait for you to see it."

"Me, either," Mom said, squeezing Norm's hand, then reaching back to rub my shoulder. "How about you, Diana? Excited?"

"Sure," I said. It was a relief to get away from school. I didn't know why, but some of the "popular" people had started talking about me. They'd started calling me "animal" in the hall when they passed. Some of the eighth-grade guys turned it into a long, ferocious sound. "Annn-i-MAL!" It had been better when they totally ignored me, when I was invisible.

But that wasn't the main reason I was excited about this trip. The main reason was I'd get to see my dad. For the first time in a year.

The bridge arched up high in the center to allow tall boats to pass underneath, and I held my breath as our car rose up, up above the water. As I looked down, a rangy boat slid under us, with two tall poles in the center and dozens of ropes and more poles set at angles from the masts, like wings.

"That's a shrimp trawler, girls," said Norm.

My jaw dropped when I looked up and took in the view. Acres of blue sky, silvery water on both sides as far as I could see, and a sliver of emerald land at the other end of the bridge. We drove down the other side of the arch, and the bridge leveled out again only a few dozen feet above the water, but it was still the longest bridge I had ever been on.

And then we were on the Outer Banks.

"When I started coming here with my family twenty years ago," Norm said, "the wild horses just wandered down the streets. There used to be a lot more."

"No way!" I said. "Wild horses?" Could it be true?

We were passing by a marina now, with line after line of sparkling, blue and white boats moored and bobbing beside the docks. On the other side of the road stood rows of beach houses with sea oats in the yards, wraparound upstairs porches, and weathered rocking chairs.

"Yep, wild horses. The story was that they were the descendants of Spanish mustangs from shipwrecks, five hundred years ago. We'd look out the window of our cottage and see them walking down the street. Several years ago people had to round them up and move them farther north because the area was becoming too populated and they were getting hit by cars."

"Hit by cars!"

"I know."

"So we can't see them anymore?"

Norm glanced at mom. "Well, I'm hoping we'll see them. Our house is on the northern part of the beach, where the horses stay."

Mom smiled back at Stephanie and me.

"Wow!" I'd always dreamed of riding a wild horse. Sometimes I dreamed I *was* one. Flying over the sand, free, no one telling me where to go or what to do. And I thought, *By the end of this week, I'll be riding a wild horse bareback on the beach.*

"Diana, look, the dunes!" Stephanie poked me again. Rising on our left were enormous mountains of sand, the biggest dunes I'd ever seen. People dotted the tops of them. Some were sand boarding, some flew kites, and we watched one guy hang glide from the top of the ridge, suspended below giant red and white wings.

"Wow!"

"That's Jockey's Ridge," Norm said. "It's the tallest sand dune on the East Coast. And right nearby is where Orville and Wilbur Wright flew the first airplane. We'll go there one day while we're here."

"Can we hang glide?"

"We'll see," Norm said. But I'd begun to recognize that tone in my stepfather's voice, which meant, *No, but I'll play along for now to pacify you, Diana.*

"How long before we get to our cottage?" Stephanie asked.

"About forty-five minutes, if the traffic isn't too bad," said Norm.

We drove for miles, past rows and rows of beach houses. On the left side, we passed a golf course, and then, on the right, a shop advertising Jet Skis and parasailing.

I thought about what it would be like to see my dad. After the divorce he moved to Florida with his girlfriend. I'd met Susan when I stayed with them for spring break last year.

This past Christmas he'd sent me fifty dollars, and he'd even called me on New Year's Day. When Mom answered the phone and said "Hello, Steven" in a suddenly stiff, defensive voice, my heart had started thumping. When I got on the phone he said he was coming to the coast of North Carolina for a conference while we would be there. So this week, I might get to see him.

We drove at least twenty more miles, passing shopping centers and more beach houses, rows and rows, some huge and new, but many small and weathered. We passed a hammock store, with hammocks hanging from trees in the front yard, and at least three WINGS stores, decorated bright yellow with blue and green waves painted along the roof line. My heart seemed to be beating faster and faster, and I could feel my Moronic Mood-o-Meter souring. Dr. Shrink had reminded me to use this stupid rating system to rate my moods, especially while we were on vacation. A ten is zooming around, out of control. One is a black cloud, depressed and angry. Five is where I want to be.

Stephanie and I were both practically hanging out the window, watching the sights go by. Since we'd crossed the bridge, we hadn't yet had a glimpse of the ocean, though I could tell from the flat land, the rows of beach houses and the salt scent in the air that it wasn't far away.

"Okay, we're in Duck now," Norm announced at one point. On our left, the sound sparkled behind a single row of shops. A huge pink plastic shark hung outside one bait shop. Shops lined the other side of the road too. In front of many shops stood statues of horses with wings, painted with wild, colorful patterns.

We passed a town called Sanderling, and a town called Corolla, which had a red brick lighthouse, and then we kept driving north. Soon we were on a narrow, windswept stretch of land that seemed to hold only the road and a few dunes with twisted, dense shrubs on either side.

"The sound is on our left, and the ocean is on our right," Norm said. "Imagine what this place is like in a storm."

"How much farther to our house?" Stephanie asked.

"Well ..." he said. "This year we're staying really far out, past the end of the road. We have to use four-wheel drive on the beach for the last bit!"

"Cool!" I said.

Stephanie didn't say anything. She chewed her fingernail.

A few miles later, the road came to an end. Norm shifted into four-wheel drive, took a right, churning through soft piles of white-rutted sand, and drove near the shoreline where waves crashed onto the flat, shimmering beach.

"Whoo-hoo!" I yelled. I leaned out of the car and let the wind whip my hair around.

"Tax season is over!" Norm joined me, leaning to his left and shouting out the window, above the roar of the wind. He's an accountant.

"Flu season is over!" Mom leaned to her right and shouted out her window. She's a physician's assistant.

Finally, Stephanie put one arm out her side and shouted, "The water looks cold!"

"I'm swimming anyway!" I shouted back, laughing.

I could tell Stephanie was scared of the horses. Last summer when we went on vacation together, we'd barely known each other. Mom had just married Norm. We'd gone to a ranch in the mountains to horseback ride, and I found out right away that riding scared Stephanie. A lot of stuff scares Stephanie.

I'd been pretty mean to Stephanie, I don't deny it. I didn't want to share Mom with Norm, and I didn't want a stepsister—especially one who is scared of everything. I went to the stables and left her alone in the cabin. I made fun of her jeans. She was scared of the horses, and I made fun of that. I even made her horse spook and run away with her.

But even though I was so mean, she was still nice to me. That surprised me. And then we'd released the wolf-dogs, and boy did we get in a lot of trouble—together. And we actually started to become friends.

Then we got home. Stephanie transferred to my school, made the eighth-grade cheerleading squad, and soon knew more people than me, even though I'd been with the same kids since fourth grade. Going on five years! Stephanie was cute and friendly and perky and perfect and didn't have to take pills.

When Stephanie and I were alone together, it was okay. At school it was different. Even though I'd always told myself I didn't care about having friends, that I'd rather be at the barn, it just wasn't fair. I was reminded once again why I liked horses more than people. Horses were nicer. They stood quietly while you brushed them, they listened to your problems, and once you climbed on their backs, your problems seemed to melt away.

Mom and Norm were always coming up with ideas to play games and go to movies when Stephanie stayed with us every other weekend. It was like having me around was normal and having her around was some special occasion or something. It really irked me. And it still drove me crazy how every little thing scared her.

Now we passed people who had parked their trucks on the beach so they could fish. The grown-ups wore tall, thick rubber boots and cast their lines out into the churning water. White plastic buckets stood on the sand beside them. Little kids wearing sweatshirts were building a sand castle that looked more like a mountain with turrets. As seagulls circled above the fishermen, hoping for scraps, their high, eerie calls pierced the air.

Driving even farther up the beach, we didn't see anyone else.

"Wow, it's deserted along here," said Mom. "That makes me a little nervous, Norm."

"Is my cell phone going to work here?" Of course Stephanie would be worried about that.

"My buddy, the guy who owns the house, said it will, honey," said Norm.

I didn't have a cell phone, but Stephanie's mom had given her one because of having to pick Stephanie up at different times from cheerleading practice. Mom and Norm had gotten annoyed with Stephanie's mom for getting her a cell phone, since I didn't have one, but I told them I didn't care. I was glad I didn't have one. If I did, people might notice that I never got a text.

It would be exciting to stay in such an isolated part of the beach. A better chance we'd see the wild horses. By the end of the week, I'd be riding bareback into the ocean. I'd always dreamed about having a horse that had never been touched by human hands but would become docile and affectionate toward me. Only me.

"I think this is where we turn," Norm said, cutting away from the water between two dunes after glancing at the directions he'd printed out. We followed a short road of packed-down sand. And back among the dunes, surrounded by sea grass and some twisted bushes leaning away from the water, were two small beach houses.

We drove slowly by a yellow house on stilts with a wraparound porch and a four-wheel-drive vehicle parked underneath. Then Norm stopped in front of a small gray cottage on stilts enclosed by latticework, with a large triangular picture window and a long, long wooden walkway leading over the dunes to the beach.

"I think this is it," Mom said, looking at the picture on the printout. "It's called Wild Horse Lookout."

"Oh, I love that name!" I said.

Stephanie glanced at the house, then over at the yellow dunes, then back to the stand of gnarled, scrubby trees with shiny leaves behind us, and bit her lip. I was reminded of the white, terrified look on her face the day her horse ran away with her. I feel bad about it now, because I laughed at her, and it had been my fault. But later I helped her with her riding, and on our last day at the ranch, she'd ridden a big, gentle gelding named Sam. Some of her fear had gone away.

Now we pulled up in front of the gray house, and the most wonderful and amazing thing happened. Seven or eight small horses, chestnut and bay and black, still wearing their rugged winter coats, galloped across the dune behind our house. Whinnying and sending sand flying, they veered away from our car and pounded off toward the inland forest. Second to last was a tiny black foal with long legs and knobby knees, stumbling along to keep up with its mother. The stallion was in the rear, also black, with his dark head low, herding the rest.

"Oh my gosh!" I practically jumped out of the car before we stopped moving. "Did you see the foal?" I couldn't believe how small the horses were. They looked like ponies. And their tails were so long they almost brushed the ground.

Mom jumped out of the car too. "Oh, Diana, wasn't that a beautiful sight?"

I ran up the dune after them, my feet sinking in the soft, cool sand, and I watched until the foal disappeared into the gnarled trees in the direction of the setting sun. Without a thought I followed her.

2

STEPHANIE

Oh my gosh, I couldn't believe those wild horses ran right through our yard! They scared me to death. At least they were smaller than the ones at the ranch last summer! After the ranch, I thought I was almost over my fear of horses. Maybe they just startled me.

I could not believe Daddy rented us this house out in the middle of nowhere. Only one other house was in sight, and it looked empty. Ever since he married Lynn, Daddy had tried to be Mr. Wild Adventureman. I guess to impress her. Well, I'm sorry, I'd known him all my life, and he was completely a city person. I wondered when that act was going to wear off, and he would let Lynn know what he was really like.

I'd already tried my cell phone. It worked. Thank God!

Of course Diana had to go running across the dunes after the wild horses.

"Diana, Stephanie, come on. We've got to unload the car!" Daddy yelled as he unhooked our two bikes from the rack on the back. I stayed around, helping him roll them under the house. He opened the rear liftgate, and I waited for him to load me down with two bags of groceries. Then I followed Lynn to the front door, where she finally got the key code to work.

"You're a big help, Stephanie," Lynn said as she pushed the door open. She put her arm around me and squeezed. "Have I gotten a chance to tell you how happy we are that you're with us?"

My face felt warm, and I couldn't stop myself from smiling. I really liked Lynn, so sometimes I felt guilty. I knew I ought to be loyal to Mama. Sometimes Mama asked me questions about Lynn, and I acted really vague. I never acted like anything I did at Dad's was fun, even though it was, because Mama would get jealous. I had been thinking and thinking about living with Daddy and Lynn. But I hadn't said it out loud to anyone.

One reason was because I really didn't like Barry's son, Matt. Matt flunked out of his first semester of college and had been living with us since Christmas because his mom said he couldn't live with her anymore. Now Mama and Barry were spending all their time arguing about what to do about him. Matt and his friends were wild, and Mama constantly tried keeping him in line, but she didn't know half of what they did. Should I tell what I knew?

But then there was Diana. Could I live with her?

I wish I could figure out where I belonged.

I heard Daddy yelling for Diana as I followed Lynn inside. The house was old-looking and comfortable, with weathered, gray porches on the front and back. Inside there were worn hardwood floors and wicker furniture with pretty but faded pillows in beachy colors, sky blue and teal. I left the grocery bags on the counter in the glaring white kitchen. White walls, appliances, countertops, cabinets, and even white bar stools. In the living room, sunlight poured in through a tall triangular window, which gave an amazing view of the royal blue sky and a long wooden walkway that led to the water over the pristine dunes.

As we were bringing in our suitcases and the rest

of the groceries, Daddy and Lynn got more and more annoyed with Diana for running off and not helping unload the car.

I dragged my suitcase upstairs, and Lynn came with me to look at the bedrooms. The master bedroom, where she and Daddy would stay, was on the first floor, but there were two small rooms on the second floor.

"Why don't you go ahead and pick whichever one you want, sweetie," Lynn said as she put towels in the bathroom. "Since she ran into the woods, Diana gave up her chance to pick." Lynn headed back downstairs.

Both rooms had yellow walls and a sliding door leading to an upstairs porch. I chose the room with a sky blue bedspread instead of the room with the navy striped comforter, and flopped my suitcase on the bed. I stepped out onto the porch and leaned over the wooden railing into the ocean breeze. I gazed at the waves and the wide, shimmering beach that stretched as far as I could see in both directions. The sky was huge, with thin wisps of silvery clouds that floated above the water like a magical land. The sun shone brightly on the dunes, and some birds flying by looked like sparkles against the clouds. So beautiful. The only problem was, there wasn't a single other person around, much less anyone my age. Except Diana, of course.

I had no idea what Daddy and Lynn would say—or Mama—about me living with them. What scared me most was asking Mama. I knew she would be so hurt. And living with Diana? Well, I would be the first to admit that I'm a "girlie girl," as in I wash and blow-dry my hair every day, and I'm particular about my clothes. Diana pays no attention to her flyaway, strawberry blonde hair. She just sticks it in a ponytail, most of the time forgets to wash it, and a lot of days doesn't even comb it. She wears jeans and sweatshirts with dirt smears (or whatever!) from the barn and doesn't care. After we'd had the adventure with the wolves last summer, I'd been happy that we'd gotten close, or at least stopped being enemies. I mean, we were stepsisters now, after all, and it meant a lot to me for us to get along.

But being in the same school changed things. I hadn't realized until I had gotten there with Diana how things were for her. She hardly had any friends, and a lot of people avoided her. She wasn't in the advanced sections of language arts like me. The only advanced section she was in was science, because the only thing she was interested in was animals. I mean, it didn't make a difference in how I felt about her. It was just, well, sometimes awkward when it came to other kids.

We both had a language arts assignment to do over spring break, which I thought was completely unfair. We both had to memorize a poem of our choice and be ready to perform it for our class when we got back. I chose a famous love poem by Elizabeth Barrett Browning called "How Do I Love Thee?"

I picked a love poem because lately I'd been thinking about love—all kinds of love—a lot. Love for another person. Love for my family. Love for God. My teacher had said, "The most powerful force in the world is love." I'd been thinking about that a lot. I wondered what it would be like when I fell in love someday.

Diana chose a poem by William Blake called "Tyger." I didn't know why it was spelled funny like that. Lynn said maybe we could practice together and perform our poems at the end of the week for her and Norm. I guess that could be kind of cool. I like poetry. When I read poems by, say, Robert Frost or Emily Dickinson, I sometimes think, *That's exactly the way I feel! How can another person know I feel that way?*

I opened my suitcase and started putting my things in the dresser drawers, automatically folding my socks and separating out my shirts and shorts like I have them arranged at home. Diana would probably live out of her suitcase the entire trip.

At school I sometimes heard people talking about Diana. Once I was standing by my locker, and I heard someone call her a name, something like "Annn-i-MAL." As I clicked my locker closed, I'd had a sick feeling in my stomach. Then I'd walked down the hall, pretending I hadn't heard anything.

The last weekend I stayed with Daddy and Lynn and Diana, I'd tried to talk to Daddy about it. I hardly ever got a chance to be alone with Daddy anymore. It had been a Saturday afternoon. Lynn had gone to pick Diana up from the barn. Dad had just finished mowing the lawn when I found him going through the mail at the kitchen counter. He had his reading glasses on, and the wrinkles between his eyes deepened as he separated the mail into piles. His T-shirt was sweaty, and there were beads of sweat on his forehead where his hair was getting thinner. I sat at the counter next to him and pretended to read the front page of the paper.

"What's up, sweetheart?" Daddy said, looking over his glasses at me with a smile.

"Nothing," I said. That's always the first thing I'd say, even if I wanted to talk about something.

"Something's on your mind." He put a bill aside and slid another out of its envelope.

"It's, well, it's Diana, I guess. She doesn't really hang out with anyone."

"Hmm." Daddy folded his glasses and put them in his shirt pocket, then he faced me. "What do you mean? Isn't she friendly with the kids that hang out at the barn?"

"I don't think so." It seemed like the horses were Diana's friends, instead of people. I crossed my legs and traced the squarish bone on top of my knee with my finger. I whispered the next part. "I heard some kids at school making fun of Diana."

Daddy sat up straighter and looked at me more sharply. "Do they bully her?"

"They talk about her behind her back."

"What kinds of things do they say?"

"They call her names. Stuff like that."

"Is she aware of it?" Daddy asked.

"I'm not sure. We've never talked about it." I couldn't tell Daddy that I hadn't stood up for Diana.

He let out a huge sigh and said, "I'll talk to Lynn about it. Meanwhile, how do you think you should handle things?"

I knew he was going to say that. "Well ... act in a loving way?" I said. "Isn't that right?" I traced my kneecap with my finger again, avoiding Daddy's eyes.

"Yes. So what should you do?"

"I guess I could invite Diana to hang out with me and my friends at school." *I'm sure that'll go over really well.*

"Good idea. You could also include her when you have friends over to the house."

"I've tried that, Dad. The one time I had Colleen over, we invited Diana to play cards, and she completely snubbed us. I mean, I could try again, but she doesn't usually want to do things with us, though."

"That's fine if she doesn't. You could just invite her, and then she can decide. Anything else?"

"I can't think of anything." That was a lie. I could think of something: Stand up for her. But I'd never do that. I couldn't even stand up for myself!

I hadn't told Dad, but I didn't invite friends over to Mama's house because of Matt, and I didn't want to invite friends over to Daddy's house because of Diana. So I just hardly ever invited anyone over.

Downstairs, cabinet doors opened and closed, and plastic grocery bags rattled. Lynn and Daddy were still unpacking the groceries.

I headed downstairs but stopped on the landing when I heard their voices starting to rise.

"Someone needs to go after her, Lynn. She could get lost in the woods."

"I don't think she'll go so far that she'll get disoriented. Diana has an excellent sense of direction. Remember the way she found her way around the ranch last summer?"

"Right after sneaking out in the middle of the night."

"Well, I'm pretty sure she won't try that again, aren't you?"

"Not sure at all, Lynn. I wouldn't put it past her to try it again. And Stephanie will go along for the ride."

"You have to trust her more, Norm."

"I will when she gives us a reason to trust her."

I stood on the steps, holding my breath, my hand on the banister. Making a decision, I went upstairs to get a sweatshirt, and then, taking a deep breath, I walked downstairs as loudly as I could.

"All unpacked?" Lynn said brightly.

"Yep," I said. "I'll go look around and find Diana."

"Well … okay," Lynn said, glancing at Daddy.

"Don't go too far," Daddy said.

"Okay." I went down the steps and through the yard, following the hoofprints of the horses in the sand. The beach grass waved in the breeze, and blowing sand hit my legs, stinging lightly.

The sound of an engine floated toward me from the beach. A boy on a beat-up, red ATV came over the dune and stopped on the path. At the summit of the dune, he took off his helmet and shook it, maybe to get sand out of it. Even from this distance, he looked very cute, with a tanned face and glasses. If he had been at my school, all the girls would have been crazy over him. He looked a little older than me.

Someone my age!

He glanced over and caught me staring. For a split second, our eyes met.

The boy replaced his helmet and pulled down the visor, then roared right by me. The wheels of the ATV blew sand on my legs. I waved at him and smiled as he drove by, just to be friendly. Then he followed the path into the woods.

As I headed for the stand of trees, the sand squeaked under my flip-flops. The trees were gnarled and squat, with long, sinuous limbs and shiny leaves. Twigs grasped at my skin, and there were burrs on the sand and prickles on every branch of every bush.

I craned my neck to see between the trees, but it was dark and tangled. The path the boy and Diana had followed turned a corner beyond a crooked tree, and I couldn't see where it went. I glanced back at the house.

Daddy was standing out on the front steps, watching me, his hands on his hips. I plunged into the woods and started down the path.

3

DIANA

I followed another turn in the path and ducked under a low-hanging pine branch. When I came out into the open, there they were, fifty yards away, gathered on a shaded grassy slope between two dunes. I stayed still and tried not to move or scare them.

They were shaggy, all right. Sturdy looking, with slim, graceful necks. Norm had said they were descendants of mustangs that swam ashore from Spanish shipwrecks. It reminded me of my favorite movie, *The*

Black Stallion. He'd been shipwrecked on that island with the boy. I thought about how the boy got to know the wild horse, and how they formed this intense relationship one tiny step at a time. Could I do that with one of these horses?

They were sorrel, chestnut, bay, and black. One of the sorrels looked almost like a palomino, light red with a blonde mane and tail. The stallion was black, like his foal. He stood highest on the dune, keeping watch, while the four mares grazed on the sea grass. The foal had his head under his mother's flank, nursing. The horses swung their long tails as if they were sweeping the ground, almost in unison, back and forth, back and forth. Such an amazing and peaceful scene. I pinched myself to make sure this was real.

I thought about picking a number for my mood and chose a four. Just about perfect.

"Hey there," I said quietly, under my breath. "How are you guys doing?"

Their ears moved a bit, but none of them laid their ears back, so I felt like they weren't that scared of me.

I thought I'd sit here in the sand watching them for a while, then slowly move closer and closer. That was what the boy in *The Black Stallion* had done. They'd get used to me being here and know I wouldn't hurt them. Maybe by the end of the week, I'd be able to ride one of them. That would be the coolest thing ever.

I watched them stand and graze, their tails swaying back and forth like metronomes, and then amble slowly from one section of grass to another.

I'd probably need to bring food to coax the horses into trusting me. I was sure Mom had brought carrots and apples.

For a long time, I just sat and watched, sliding closer every few minutes or so until I was about fifteen feet away. I was close enough to see the grass tremble near their nostrils as they grazed. The foal, my favorite, had begun to nurse again.

The sun shone in my eyes. Seagull cries wafted through the air. The rhythmic crunch of the horses eating the grass filled my ears, and the scent of the horses floated over to me. I picked up a handful of sand and let it fall through my fingers like an hourglass. Was it possible to be any happier?

Then I heard a noise behind me. I turned around. Stephanie!

I held my finger to my mouth. "Shhh!"

Stephanie's mouth was hanging open. She didn't come any closer at first, and I could tell the horses scared her. Well, too bad. I turned back to watch them, trying to think of a name for the foal. Maybe a Spanish name, since the horses were descended from Spanish mustangs.

"Diana!" Stephanie whispered. She came a few steps closer and knelt on the sand. "I came to get you. Daddy and Lynn didn't know where you were."

"Tell them I'm right here." *Duh.*

"They want you to come back. They want you to unpack your stuff."

The horses' ears twitched. Gradually they started moving away from us. Though you could hardly notice the slow, casual way they drifted away.

"You're making them leave!" I hissed at her.

"Sorry."

The horses were even farther away now.

"I might not ever see these horses again. This might be my only chance."

"I'll stay just a minute." Stephanie shrugged and sat down beside me. "Aww, that foal looks like a little angel," she said. "A little dark angel."

"Dark Angel," I said. Stephanie could be annoying, but I grudgingly admitted that was a pretty good name.

But now the stallion decided he wanted to move the herd. He walked behind the others with his head lowered and urged them ahead. I had seen the geldings at the barn do this with mares, and Josie, our barn manager, had explained it to me. The horses' compact bodies slid between the trees, and in a few minutes the whole herd had disappeared into the forest. Dark Angel too.

I yanked up some grass and threw it on the ground. "Thanks a lot, Stephanie."

"Look, I'm sorry," Stephanie said. "I don't want Daddy and Lynn to get mad at us."

I stood up, kicking sand. I headed back toward the house without looking back at her. She caught up with me. "I just don't want things to be bad on our vacation."

"Leave me alone!" I stomped through the stand of pines and prickly bushes, pushing branches out of my way, trying to leave her behind.

Before we went back to school, Stephanie really tried hard to get along with me. But once she got to school and started making new friends, she stopped trying as hard.

One of the things I always heard people saying about Stephanie was that she was nice to everyone, and that was true. I'd never seen her be mean. And sometimes that drove me crazy. Sometimes I just felt crummy and felt like being mean. How could she be nice all the time? And then I wondered, is she just being nice to me because she's always nice, or does she really care about me? Last summer, when we'd helped the wolves, I had been pretty sure she really cared, but after watching her with people at school, I wasn't so sure.

When I told Dr. Shrink about it, she said maybe the

reason I thought people didn't like me was because of my insecurities about my dad, since he was always letting me down. So I was always waiting for other people—like Stephanie, and my mom—to let me down too. "Diana, do you think that maybe sometimes you are testing people?" Dr. Shrink asked once.

I thought about it a minute. "What if I am?" I asked. But now, at last, Dad wasn't letting me down. I was really going to visit him in just a few days. And it was going to be different this time.

Stephanie and I headed out of the woods and into the open just as the sound of motors bore down on us, increasing in volume. And then two ATVs screamed by, both carrying guys in jeans. They weren't wearing helmets. One guy had a buzz cut, and the other had wavy blond hair.

"Whoo-hoo!" both riders yelled when they saw us. The first guy lifted the front two wheels of his vehicle a few inches into the air.

"Whoa!" Stephanie cried as we jumped back to keep from getting pelted with sand. Then we dashed down the path, back toward our house, scraping our arms and legs on the prickly bushes. We ran until we were gasping for breath. Finally we slowed to a walk.

"Well, that was rude!" Stephanie said.

Now we were coming more out into the open, close

enough to see the rooftops of the two houses in our little area, and we heard a motor approaching again.

Around the corner, from the direction of the beach, careened another sandy, mud-splashed, red ATV. This rider was thin and was wearing a gray T-shirt, jeans, and running shoes. He passed us, the roar of the ATV motor exploding in our ears, sand churning out behind him in an angry cloud. His helmet made him look like a bird of prey.

"Him again," said Stephanie, wiping sand off her arms.

Looking at the curve of his back as he went by, I could practically count his ribs through his T-shirt. The bottoms of his jeans were wet, so he must have been riding in the surf.

"That's a different guy," I said.

"I know. I saw him when I started looking for you."

We continued past a grassy dune and down the sandy, rutted road toward our house. The boy had pulled up beside the yellow house next to ours and took off his helmet.

"That must be where he's staying," Stephanie said.

He had wavy, black hair and wore glasses. Something about the slimness and curve of his neck reminded me of the wild horses. He looked a little older than we were.

When we walked by, Stephanie waved at him, and

after a second's hesitation, he waved back. Then he turned away, hooking the helmet under the seat of the ATV.

"I guess you're friends already?" I said sarcastically. When we were at the mountain ranch, Stephanie had met a guy in, like, five minutes.

"No, I just think it's nice to wave, that's all." Stephanie glanced at me with a look of surprise. She pulled a long piece of her dark hair over her shoulder and twirled it between her fingers. "I think he wants to get to know us. Otherwise, why did he drive so close to us and spray us with sand?"

"Because he's a jerk?"

Stephanie laughed and danced a little beside me. "I think he's cute."

"Stephanie! He looks older than us." I looked at the sand beneath my feet, watching my flip-flops. I realized the little dance had been for the boy's benefit.

"So?"

I could feel her beside me, still acting like she thought he was watching her. I was so embarrassed! I could feel myself turning red and was glad when we had passed safely by.

The sun dropped lower in the sky, and the shadows on the sand grew longer. We climbed the stairs to our house, but both of us, at the same time, looked back in the direction of the boy before we went inside. He was gone.

"There you are," Mom said as soon as we got inside. She folded empty grocery bags and put them in a drawer. "You can't run off like that, Diana."

"I just wanted to see the wild horses."

Norm came out of the bedroom carrying the camera bag. "Diana, this is not a very populated area, especially since we're here in the off-season. You shouldn't wander around following those horses without telling us where you're going."

"That's right, sweetie," Mom broke in. "Who knows what could happen, and we don't even know if our cell phones work."

"Mine does," Stephanie said. "I checked."

"Everyone is unpacked except you, Diana," Norm said. "Why don't you unpack your stuff?"

I walked over to the window and stared out at the sand and water. Just because Norm said I had to do something didn't mean I had to do it.

"I'll do it later," I said.

I didn't look at him, but I could feel the waves of anger coming off of him. I just stared out the window, pretending he wasn't there.

"Why don't you do it now," he said. But it wasn't a question.

Now he was turning this into a standoff. What difference did it make if I unpacked now or later? All he wanted to do was show that he had power over me. I couldn't stand that. Nobody had power over me. If only I could be like the wild horses, going wherever I pleased whenever I pleased.

I waited for Mom to intervene, taking my side, the way she usually did, but instead she took his side, which was humiliating.

"Come on, Diana," she said. "Go upstairs and unpack your stuff."

"We can either have a good vacation or a bad vacation; the decision is up to you," Norm said.

"Thanks for bringing her back, Stephanie," Mom said.

Mom tapped her temple in the signal we'd developed with my doctor to tell me to think about what I was doing. I pretended I didn't see her do it. Of course, Stephanie was their perfect little daughter, and I was the bad one.

More and more, Mom and Norm were ganging up on me.

"Come on, Diana, I'll go upstairs with you," Stephanie said. "I picked one of the rooms, but see which one you like better."

Without talking to anyone, I started up the stairs

with my suitcase. I would show them. Maybe they'd wake up one morning here at the beach and find me gone. Maybe I'd go live with the wild horses. Maybe they'd have to call the police and comb the beach for miles around. Or maybe I would just go live with Dad. Norm would feel guilty for being so hard on me. Stephanie would wish she'd been a better stepsister, and Mom would be heartbroken.

4

STEPHANIE

I followed Diana to the top of the stairs.

"I picked the room with the blue bedspread, but I don't really care that much which room I get if you want it," I said. I really wanted us to get along on this trip.

Diana, without answering, went into the room with the striped bedspread and dumped everything in her suitcase on top of the bed. "Okay, I'm officially unpacked," she said.

"Right," I said, laughing, thinking that maybe we'd

just avoided a big fight. But then she walked to the door of her room and slammed it.

Sigh. Life with Diana.

I had already hung my sundress in the small closet and folded my T-shirts and shorts in the dresser. Opening the sliding door, I stepped onto the wooden upper porch overlooking the beach and ocean, and then leaned on the railing, watching and listening to the hushed sound of the waves beyond the dunes. I loved that sound. It just made me feel happy in my skin. Birds sang loudly, though I couldn't see them. From below, strains of classical guitar floated up from one of Daddy's CDs. A breeze threaded through my hair.

Through the sliding door to her room, I could see Diana lying on her bed on her stomach, on top of her clothes.

She had to be mad at Daddy for yelling at her.

"Hey," I called, "it's cool that we have this porch to ourselves."

Diana didn't answer. She remained on her bed without moving.

There were a lot of times when the three of us—Daddy and Lynn and I—were all working to get Diana to cooperate. It reminded me of when we were at the ranch last summer, and one of the horses was running around the ring bucking, and three wranglers were trying to lasso it all at the same time.

Maybe if I were bad, Daddy would pay me attention, like he did with Diana, or like Mama and Barry did with Matt. How is it fair that Diana gets to live with Daddy all the time, and I only see him every other week? He's not even her father.

One of the only times I'd been by myself with Daddy since he married Lynn was last week at Easter, when we went to the Methodist church at the last minute. My friend Colleen had told me the youth group was fun, and she'd invited me to come before the church service on Easter.

Daddy had come to pick me up, and when we passed the church, he got a funny look on his face. He turned to me and said, "Hey, Steph, want to go? Just you and me? Lynn took Diana to the barn, and they won't be back until later."

When I was little, I used to go to church with Daddy and Mama, but we hadn't been in a long time, since before the divorce. "Okay," I'd said.

The service was more modern than our old church, and had a band with guitars and microphones instead of a choir with robes. In her sermon, the preacher talked about how Jesus's resurrection can bring about a resurrection in each one of us. A whole new life. Daddy had taken my hand and squeezed it, and suddenly I realized there was a tear rolling down his cheek.

After the service, we went to lunch. "I didn't realize

how much I missed going to church," Daddy had told me while we ate.

It had been a beautiful, warm day. The daffodils and dogwoods were blooming everywhere. I watched a family of four walk by outside the restaurant, with two little kids in their pastel Easter outfits. The boy had on a pink bow tie.

"Diana doesn't believe in God," I had told Daddy. I turned to watch his face. He wiped his mouth with his napkin before saying anything. "Did she tell you that?" he asked. I couldn't tell what he was thinking from his expression.

"Yes."

"Did she say why?"

"She said one time she heard a story about a barn catching on fire. All the horses inside died. She said how could God let such a thing happen? He could have stopped it. So she decided there was no such thing as God."

"I see," he had said, turning his coffee cup around in his hands. "Well, what about you? Do you believe in God?"

I watched Daddy's face while I considered. "What about *you*, Daddy? Do you still believe in God?" Had Daddy stopped believing in God? Maybe because God didn't prevent the divorce?

Daddy blew out a heavy breath. "I can see why you might wonder," he had said. "I guess I've been angry with God. But yes, I believe in him."

"Me too," I said. And that was all we had said about it. I was surprised he hadn't seemed shocked about Diana, and it made me want to open up more. I wanted to tell him about what had happened with Matt. I really wished Matt wouldn't live with Mama and Barry and me anymore.

Matt and his friends were always on the computer, going on Facebook and laughing. Once I tried to see what they were doing, and Matt said, "Get out of here, you little twerp!" I was so shocked and embarrassed, tears came to my eyes and I could hardly see where I was going when I left the room. I had tried not to cry as heat crept up my neck and face. The laughter of Matt and his friends followed me out of the room, burning my ears.

Another time I got dropped off from cheerleading when Mama and Barry were out, and Matt and his friends were drinking beer in the basement. I hadn't told Mama. I could imagine what Matt would have said to me then. *Crybaby! Tattletale!* After that, I stayed away from Matt. I wanted to tell Daddy. I had the perfect chance to tell him at brunch after church that day. I could've asked him then if I could live with him and Lynn. But I chickened out. I was afraid of hurting Mama's feelings. I was afraid Daddy would say no.

Then the chance passed, and I went back home to Mama's house.

Now I had a whole week with Daddy and Lynn. If everything went okay this week, I promised myself I'd ask them.

Diana came out onto the porch. She didn't say anything, and her eyes were still dark and angry. She leaned on the railing a few feet away from me, looking down at the porch below. I could see her measuring the distance from this porch to the one below.

She glanced sideways at me. "Let's sneak out tonight and find the horses," she said. "If we wait till Mom and Norm go to bed, they'll never hear us." If I was going to ask Daddy about living with him this week, I wasn't going to take any chances of getting into trouble. "No way! Remember how much trouble we got into last summer?"

"How could they catch us? We'll be back before they wake up. They'll never know."

"I don't want to get in trouble."

"I don't want to get in trouble." Diana mocked me in a baby voice then. She looked at me and shook her head with disgust.

Just then someone came out onto the beach from the

path beside our house. It was the skinny, dark-haired boy who had been riding the red ATV. He wore beat-up running shoes with no socks, longish nylon shorts, and a sleeveless hoodie. Diana and I watched without speaking as he went down to the hard, dark sand near the edge of the water, did a few stretches, put in his earbuds and then took off running. Like a soldier, he pounded down the beach.

"How old do you think he is?" I asked.

"Fifteen? Sixteen? He's fast," Diana said.

Diana joined our school cross country team this year, at Daddy's urging. Daddy told us everybody should try one sport a year. Diana tried to quit after the first week of practice, but Daddy wouldn't let her.

Turns out she was good. The stands were always full for our football and basketball games, but hardly any-body went to cross country meets. At the first meet, Dad, Lynn, and I basically stood around the finish line with a few parents and siblings. After we waited what seemed like forever, the leaders burst out of the woods. All the really fast boys came thundering across the finish line, panting and soaked in sweat. And moments later, there came Diana, with her thin, white legs; spiky, strawberry blonde ponytail; and flaming red spots on her pale, freckled cheeks. Even without decent running shoes, Diana was the fastest girl. I was shocked to see her first, especially since she claimed to hate it so much.

I couldn't believe how much Daddy and Lynn cheered for her. I wished they would cheer half as much for me when I was at a cheerleading competition. I mean, I'm balancing on people's fingertips, and she's *running*.

Anyway, Daddy and Lynn took her out after that first meet and got her some good running shoes with blue and orange stripes. By the end of the season, she had put all kinds of miles on those shoes, and she'd come in first for the girls at every meet. She still complained and said she hated it, but she admitted she loved the way running helped her mood.

I looked over at Diana, who was watching the boy. He had run so far down the beach by now that he was a tiny moving dot. The late afternoon wind had picked up, whipping our clothes and hair.

"Hey, want to go for a walk on the beach?" I asked Diana.

"I know why you said that," she said, looking at the dot. "But sure." We each grabbed a sweatshirt and headed downstairs.

5

DIANA

I didn't feel like talking to Mom and Norm, so I let Stephanie tell them we were going for a walk on the beach. They told us not to go swimming since they weren't going to be down there with us, and we told them that the water was cold enough to turn us into giant goose bumps anyway.

Mom, in the kitchen starting dinner, gave me a searching, intense look, but I ignored her. She said something about what time she wanted us home. Mom was letting her blonde hair grow out a little bit because Norm liked it longer. I thought Mom ought to wear her hair however she wanted, not the way Norm wanted. Framed by the longer waves, her face looked softer now than it used to. Before she married Norm, when it was just the two of us, Mom's face had looked so pointed and tense.

Norm was inserting a bunch of his oldie CDs into the player provided at the house. He drove me crazy listening to Bruce Springsteen and Jackson Browne and other rockers who were about a million years old. He did have a CD by Tracy Chapman that I liked. She sang in a throaty voice about a revolution and the world changing, and it made me want to believe her. One of these days people would stop telling me what to do all the time.

Stephanie and I went onto the back porch and headed down the long wooden walkway to the beach. Small dunes dotted with clumps of grasses on either side of the walkway swayed in the salty sea breeze. Right beside the walkway a sign proclaimed Do Not Disturb the Dunes. Just ahead, the surf roared with a soothing rhythm.

Stephanie's long, dark hair kept blowing in her eyes, so she took a rubber band from her wrist and pulled her hair back into a ponytail. In the humidity, her hair had begun to curl around her face. My hair doesn't do anything.

At the end of the walkway, we stepped onto the sand and both turned left, into the wind, in the direction of the running boy.

"He ran into the wind first," I said, "so running back will be easier, with the wind at his back." I ran down to the shoreline, digging in with my toes as the water foamed over my feet, leaving me ankle deep in the dark, wet sand. The water was so cold it made my feet ache. "It's freezing!" When I ran out, I noticed my feet had turned bright red.

Stephanie came down, dipped one polished toe in the racing froth, started to squeal, and then ran out again.

We passed a small patch of sand nestled in the dunes that had been roped off with orange tape attached to some stakes. A small sign attached to one of the stakes warned against disturbing the area.

"Look!" Stephanie said as she stopped. "Sea turtle eggs are buried here. One night this summer when the moon is full, a bunch of baby turtles will hatch and crawl down to the sea. I went to a program about the sea turtles one summer when we were here."

"I've heard of those," I said quickly. Mom and I had not been on many vacations before she married Norm. Sometimes we'd take day trips, but never a real vacation like this one, or like last summer at the ranch. I stooped to pick up a broken piece of shell, then told Stephanie what was on my mind. "I know Norm is your dad and you love him, but he's always trying to tell me what to do. He's not my father."

"But at least you get to be with him," Stephanie said then. "I only get to see him every other week."

I didn't answer for a minute. I'd never thought of that. Then I said, "Well, I hardly ever see him."

"Still. I'm not going to say that my dad cares more about you than your own dad," Stephanie said, "because I know that'll make you mad. I haven't even met your dad. But sometimes I wish you'd try to look at things from another person's point of view. My dad feels responsible for you. He's not trying to be your dad; he's just trying to help you. I think you should be grateful that he cares."

"I don't need a lecture. I don't want to talk about this anymore." I shouldn't have brought it up. I should have known she'd say stuff like this. Anger pulsed through my body. "If I sneak out, are you going to tell on me?" I narrowed my eyes, shaking back my blowing hair.

"Did I tell on you last summer?" Stephanie shot back. She walked ahead and wiped her eyes. Was she crying? I pretended not to notice.

Just then we saw someone far up the beach examining something in the sand.

"Wonder if that's him," Stephanie said. As we got closer, we saw that it was the boy, in his sleeveless hoodie, bending over to look at something.

"What's he looking at?" I said.

As we walked closer, my heart began to beat faster. I realized I was counting on Stephanie to be the one to say something to him, because she was the one who made friends so easily. I hated boys.

He was looking at a dead man o' war. It lay glistening like a bluish-pink balloon in the sand, with tentacles tangled beside it like purple and blue spaghetti.

While I was trying to think about how to walk by, or whether he would notice us, Stephanie just walked up beside him, looked down, and said, "Eww, what is that?"

He looked up and held out his thin, muscled arm, preventing her from coming closer. "Careful, it can still sting." He had piercing, dark brown eyes, and his face was narrow, with a sharp nose. He moved with quick, precise energy. With the knuckle of his index finger, he pushed his glasses up on his nose.

"A man o' war, right?" I said.

"Yeah. Don't touch it. It can still sting for up to a week after it's dead."

"A week?" Stephanie said. "That's amazing."

"It's not just one creature; it's actually a colony made

of four different kinds of polyps that all need each other. See the four different kinds?" He pointed to one after another.

"How do you know all that?" Stephanie asked.

"I've studied a bunch of animals. My mother is a botanist. She's here doing research on the maritime forest." He stood and took a look at Stephanie, then turned to me. I studied my toes, hoping my blush didn't show. His gaze was so direct. "You staying in the gray house?"

"Yeah, we are," Stephanie said. "You're in the yellow one? With the ATV?"

"Yeah, but the ATV isn't ours. It belongs to the owner of the house. He lets us use it."

"Do you run cross country?" Stephanie asked. "My stepsister, Diana, runs cross country for our school. She said you're pretty fast."

It amazed me the way Stephanie was able to strike up a conversation. Me, I couldn't say a thing to him.

"Yeah." The boy nodded, then looked over at me. "What distance are you running?"

I managed to mumble, "3K."

"So you're in eighth grade?"

I nodded. For some reason, I couldn't seem to find my tongue.

"I'm in tenth grade, running for my high school, so I'm running the 5K."

"How old are you?" Stephanie asked.

"Sixteen. I got my license two months ago." He smiled, flashing white teeth.

"Do you live in North Carolina?" Stephanie asked.

"Yeah. Raleigh. What about you?"

"We're from Charlotte," Stephanie said. "Are you going back to the house?"

"Yeah."

"So are we," she said.

We all started walking back together.

"So, you're into science?" Stephanie asked. "What did you do for your eighth grade science project?"

I was impressed. How did she know how to ask questions like this?

"Bioluminescence," he said.

"What's that?" Stephanie asked.

He tossed a shell into the ocean. "Well, it's light that's produced by living things. Like lightning bugs. I did my project on organisms in the ocean."

"Oh. How do they do it, anyway?"

"Well, when some organisms are under stress—like being thrown around in the waves—they put off light. I'm hoping maybe I'll see it while I'm here."

"Cool," Stephanie said.

"How exactly do they put off light?" I finally got up the nerve to ask a question.

He waved his arm, as if to dismiss the question. "It's probably too complicated for you to understand."

I felt heat rising to my face. "That's an arrogant thing to say! How do you know we won't understand?"

"Well, maybe it would just take too long to explain," Stephanie said quickly, obviously trying to smooth things over. That's what she always does. Tries to smooth things over.

"I have time," I said, stopping on the beach and glaring at him. "Tell me. How exactly do animals put off light?"

He looked a little surprised, then stopped and said, in a kind of sarcastic voice, "The enzyme luciferase creates a chemical reaction that changes luciferin plus oxygen to oxyluciferin plus light. Got it?"

I walked as fast as I could ahead of them. What a jerk! The sun had dropped lower in the sky, the tide had come in, and the beach had shrunk and narrowed since we left the cottage. I started up the walkway to our house.

"Maybe we'll see you tomorrow," Stephanie said, apparently not realizing that I personally didn't care if I ever saw him again.

"That would be excellent."

"Oh … my name is Stephanie, and that's Diana. What's your name?"

"Cody."

"Well, maybe we'll see you tomorrow, Cody," Stephanie said.

"Okay, maybe."

I glanced back in time to watch him saunter away with a small salute.

I kept going up the walkway and didn't say a word.

Stephanie followed me in silence. Finally I stopped and turned around. She looked at me with raised eyebrows.

"He's not going to see *me* tomorrow," I said. "I can't believe you kept being nice to him. He said we wouldn't understand! Like we're stupid or something."

I planned to never speak to him again.

6

STEPHANIE

"I think Cody just thought that we wouldn't know the scientific terms," I told Diana as we climbed onto the back porch. "I don't hold it against him. I thought he was cute."

Diana stopped and looked at me with her hands on her hips. "He talked to us like we were idiots," she said.

"He was just passionate about what he likes. I don't know why you're mad at him."

Lynn poked her head out the back door. "Hi, girls.

We're going to eat outside on the porch. Could you set the table, please?"

I set the wooden table out there, quickly placing the forks on top of the napkins so they wouldn't blow away. Diana, as usual, didn't help. *Maybe if they see how helpful I am, they'll want me to live with them.* Daddy brought the speakers outside so we could listen to music, and he let me put on Taylor Swift. I loved her album *Fearless* because she sang about being afraid too. She said being "fearless" means having the courage to live your life in spite of the fear.

I wished I wasn't afraid of so many things. Horses. Terrible loud fights like the ones Mama and Daddy used to have. The fights that Mama and Barry had now about Matt.

We sat out on the porch, peeling and eating shrimp that Lynn and Daddy picked up from a roadside stand, and listening to the music and the ocean, with the seagulls circling above us.

"Look at the pelicans," Lynn said, pointing up. Seven of the big, dark birds flew over us in a stately fashion, in a perfectly straight line, their wings frozen in position. They looked almost like ships flying through the air. Then, one after the other, like dominoes, they each flapped their wings three times.

Diana was quiet and sulking at dinner. Last summer,

when we were at the ranch, the way Diana acted really upset me, but I was learning to stop letting it bother me.

"We met the boy that's staying in the yellow house," I said to Daddy and Lynn. "He's sixteen and runs cross country, like Diana."

"You girls didn't waste any time getting to know someone!" Lynn exclaimed. "What's this boy like?"

"I didn't like him!" Diana said, tossing a shrimp shell onto her plate. "He said that Stephanie and I are too stupid to understand bioluminescence."

"That's not really what he said," I argued.

"Where's he from?" Daddy asked.

"Raleigh," I said.

"Well, I'm glad you girls met a friend," Lynn said.

"He acted like he thought he was better than us!" Diana said.

"He may have said that as a defense mechanism," Lynn said, "just to boost his confidence while talking to new people. You yourself sometimes say things you don't mean when you're feeling insecure, right?"

Diana focused on shelling a shrimp and didn't answer.

After dinner we put on sweatshirts and took flashlights and walked on the beach. Now that the sun had gone down, the sand felt cool. Daddy put his arm around my shoulder and aimed the flashlight beam on sand crabs that frantically scuttled sideways to escape our feet. Lynn tried to take Diana's hand, but she pulled her hand away and walked alone a little distance away from us. Then Lynn came and walked with Daddy's other arm around her. So it was me and Daddy and Lynn together, and Diana all by herself. Well, it was Diana's choice. What's her deal?

When we got back to the house, Lynn pulled a worn box off the bookshelf. "Hey, look! They have a Pictionary game! Let's play. Steph, want to be my partner? You and me against Diana and Norm." She put the box on the kitchen table and started taking out the playing pieces and cards.

"Okay!" I helped Lynn place the pencils and notepads around the table. I don't want to lie: I'm good at drawing clues, and my team wins a lot. I love board games.

"Lynn, my wonderful bride, why in the world don't you want me on your team?" Daddy said. He wrapped his arms around her as she opened the board.

"Because nobody can even tell what your drawings are, my sweet love," Lynn said, laughing.

"Hey, I'm what you call a minimalist," Daddy protested. "It's my style."

"It's what I call a hopeless scribble!" I said, laughing.

"Enough of that!" Daddy said, chuckling. "We'll take them on, won't we, Diana?"

"I don't want to play," Diana said, starting up the stairs.

"Come on, it'll be fun," Lynn said.

"We'll all play," Norm said. "We can do this, Diana, no problem. With your outstanding drawings and my excellent guessing. "

"I. Don't. Want. To." She went upstairs and shut the bedroom door.

You can't play Pictionary with three. Was Daddy going to make her play? Were we going to have a huge fight? Was she mad because Lynn had asked me to be on her team? I couldn't believe Diana was going to ruin this.

I stopped what I was doing, holding my breath.

Lynn looked at Daddy, raised her eyebrows, and started putting the pieces back in the box. Daddy looked upstairs at the closed door and then seemed to make a decision.

"Do they have a deck of cards in that drawer? You can play hearts with three," he said. "Stephanie, we'll have to teach Lynn to play."

If he was upset, he was doing a good job not showing it. Lynn found some cards, and we sat at the table.

"The object of the game is to have the lowest score,"

said Daddy, fanning out the cards so Lynn could see. "Each heart you take counts one point against you. And there are two special cards—the queen of spades and the jack of diamonds. The jack is good—ten points subtracted from your score. The queen is bad—thirteen points added to your score."

"So you want the jack, but you don't want the queen, right?" Lynn asked.

"Correct," Daddy said. "Ready?"

We started playing, and at first we were quiet, with Daddy and me instructing Lynn on strategies of the game. Then Daddy dumped the queen of spades on one of Lynn's tricks, and she said, "Oh, Norm, how can you do such a terrible thing to me?"

Daddy laughed and said, "Every man for himself," the way he does when we play games.

During the next game, Lynn slapped the queen on Daddy.

"Take that!" she said.

"You sure caught on quick!" Daddy said, pretending to be hurt.

"So sorry!" Lynn said.

And pretty soon we were shrieking with laughter, yelling, and pounding the table. We forgot all about Diana. At one point, while we were playing, I looked up and saw her sitting on the stairs, watching us. The moment I saw her, she got up and disappeared into her room.

I normally like sleeping late, but the next morning, bright April sun spilled into my bedroom and woke me early. I opened my eyes, listening to the *shhh-shhh* sound of the surf. I stretched, feeling deliciously relaxed.

I lay there for a few minutes, listening. We were going to be here for a whole week, waking up and hearing this every single morning. And we were going to be walking on the beach, letting the sand sift through our toes every day.

When Mama and Daddy were still married, here at this beach was one place they always seemed happy. Mama used to sit on the back deck putting polish on her toes, listening to her music, and drinking Diet Coke. She sat on the beach and rubbed oil on herself and focused on her tan. Daddy used to play with me and toss me into the surf, or let me bury him in the sand. Sometimes he'd fish, and mostly he didn't catch anything, but once in a while he'd catch a small, bony flounder or cod.

This week would be different. Lynn wore 50 SPF sunscreen. She brought a broad, blue and white umbrella, a fat nonfiction book about sea turtles, and a pair of binoculars so she could look for dolphins. She and Daddy made a lot of plans for this week. I think one day, maybe even today, they were going to go play golf together. They had planned for another day of sightseeing. I was sure Diana would try to find the horses, and there was bound to be a lot of drama, because wherever Diana is, there's drama.

I knew I had to leave memories behind. And it was okay. Mama and Daddy didn't get along at home, and we were only at the beach for one week a year. You couldn't have a life when you only got along for one week a year. But still I thought about it, about the three of us together. The music playing, the smell of the ocean, Mama's nail polish, and Daddy's grilling.

I knew that there were a lot of kids just like me, adjusting to living in two places, and it was practically normal, the new normal, really. And it was fine; I was fine. Most of the time I felt lucky to have two families.

I'd met Colleen at school this year, who lived with her dad and stepmom. Her mom had been killed in a car crash when she was really little. Colleen told me she didn't love her stepmom at first. In fact, she hated her. I told her it had been easy for me to love Lynn but not Diana.

On the back porch, I leaned over the railing, and the sun warmed my hair. The light reflected off the sand and the water in the most wonderful golden way. Today it was already warmer than yesterday. And there were already about five people out on the beach. Cody's yellow house looked quiet, with the red ATV parked in the driveway.

I peeked into Diana's room and breathed a sigh of relief. She was still there, asleep. The striped comforter had slid onto the floor. Either she hadn't snuck out, or she was already back.

Thirty minutes later, I was standing by the sliding door in my bikini, with my beach bag over my shoulder, ready to go out onto the beach, and Diana was shoveling Cheerios into her mouth.

"Norm and I are going to play golf today," Lynn said as she finished loading the breakfast dishes into the dishwasher. "We'll be gone for about five hours, and we're trusting you girls to show that you're mature enough to stay on your own for a while. Can you do that?"

Diana nodded enthusiastically, still shoveling. None of us had said a word about her not playing games with us last night. We acted like nothing had happened.

Lynne and Daddy were going to be gone almost the

whole day. I could tell Diana was ecstatic but trying to act very calm at the same time. My mouth felt dry.

"Now, I want you girls to put on sunscreen before going down on the beach."

Daddy came out of the bedroom wearing his favorite green Masters golf hat. He carried his golf shoes as well as Lynn's. Lynn hadn't played golf until she met Daddy. Daddy said she'd picked up the game really fast, but Lynn kept saying she wasn't very good.

"And no swimming," he said, "since we won't be here."

"Daddy, the water's freezing," I said. "We'd have to be crazy to go in."

"And you can hang around the house and on the beach area nearby, but no wandering off looking for horses or anything like that," Lynn said. She pulled her hair into a thin ponytail and slid on her golf visor. "Understand, Diana?" She raised her eyebrows.

"Yes." Diana didn't make eye contact with Lynn.

"Okay, give me a hug," Lynn said. She wrapped her arms around me, patting me on the back a few times, and then moved the Cheerios box and hugged Diana, kissing the top of her head. Diana focused on balancing a spoonful of Cheerios, ignoring her.

"All right," Norm said, his hand on the door handle. "We'll call from the turn. Hey, maybe you could even start memorizing your poems for school today."

"Oh, Daddy!" I said.

"Well, you've got to do it sometime. Anyway, if things go well today, we'll be much more likely to trust you girls to be on your own later in the week."

"Have a good game," I said.

The door slammed. The minute the car started down below, Diana threw her spoon into the air. "Yes! Five hours alone!"

"Whoo-hoo!" I said, trying to sound enthusiastic. But what would Diana do? "Are you going down to the beach?" I asked her. "I'll wait for you if you want."

"That's okay," she said. "You go ahead."

I stared at her. "Aren't you going to come down?"

"Sure," she said. "Later."

I was sure Diana was up to something. She always was. I almost said something to her. But then I decided, *I'm just not going to, I'm just going to go down on the beach and read my book.* Maybe Cody would come talk to me.

"See you down there," I said.

7

DIANA

I went upstairs and put on shorts, a T-shirt, and running shoes. This was my chance. Downstairs, I got a bottle of water and took a big swig. Then I stuffed a couple of apples and carrots into a plastic bag and went out the front door, jogging down the path toward where I'd last seen the horses.

Eventually, Stephanie would figure out that I wasn't coming. I would be back before Mom and Norm got back from golf, and they would never know. I probably wouldn't even have to go that far.

In *The Black Stallion*, the boy had taken a long time to get close to the stallion. Today, I had five whole hours. I could accomplish a lot in that time.

I hurried through the first stand of gnarled trees, ignoring the way the branches seemed to reach out and claw at me like long-fingered arms. As I ran along, moving farther from the beach, the soil changed. Underneath the top layer of white sand, the soil was dark and loamy.

The path wound around a few curves, leading deeper into the forest. An SUV passed me, and I kept running. It was warmer today, and I was soon sweating.

I thought about the last time I'd seen Dad, over last year's spring break. The thought of seeing him made my chest tighten and my cheeks go hot. How would he be? Would he be in one of his jovial, funny moods? Would he pay attention to me, or ignore me, like last time? I had told myself that it was cool last time I visited, because he let me do anything I wanted. I asked if I could taste his beer, and he told me I could have one. I got one out of the fridge, but then I took one taste and changed my mind. Another time I wanted to walk to a shopping center down the highway, and he didn't say a word about it being dangerous. Then Stephanie said he probably let me do that because he was basically ignoring me.

Why did I care so much about making him notice me, anyway?

Mom had told me a million times not to get my hopes up about him calling. But it seemed like this time he had sounded different.

When I got to a jagged Y-shaped piece of driftwood, I angled farther from the water and deeper into the maritime forest. The scrub pines, yaupon bushes, and live oaks became thicker. I slowed way down because running was a lot harder. Some of the sand was deep, and large puddles had formed across the beaten-down road.

My lungs burned. My calves ached. A damp coating of sweat and salt covered my entire body. I hadn't realized how much longer this was than my usual cross country course. And it was late morning, a fairly stupid time to run, if I did say so myself.

But no matter how much my muscles hurt after a run, my mood was always fantastic. About a ten on the Moronic Mood-o-Meter. On days we had cross country practice, I sometimes forgot to take my mood pills. I started feeling so good, I didn't need them, like a kind of cool brain buzz, like right now. I felt like nothing could stop me.

It had been almost a full day since I'd seen the horses. They could be miles away. But I was counting on them being out around here somewhere. I wouldn't give up until I found them.

Pretty soon I had to slow down to a walk. The sand had turned fluffy, and it sucked my feet down into it like a drain. Panting, and pushing sweaty tendrils of hair back from my face, I finally found the packed-down road we'd been on yesterday. I climbed it to the top of a dune. And before me lay rolling sand hills dotted with the small scrub pines and sea grasses that the wild horses had learned to eat.

Off to my right stood some houses on stilts with old, faded looking cars sitting outside. Nailed to trees around the yards were black and red signs reading No Trespassing and Keep Out.

No horses anywhere.

At the top of the next dune, I sat down, took off my shoes, and poured a bunch of sand out of each one.

I put my shoes back on and wandered farther. The sun blazed above me, and away from the water the breeze died away to nothing, so the air sat heavy as a blanket. My mouth felt like cotton, and my teeth gritted on sand. When beads of sweat rolled out of my hair and into my eyes, I swiped them away, but it didn't stop the burning.

I decided to walk over one more dune. See what was on the other side. If I didn't see anything, I'd turn back.

There! Gathered in the shade of a huge live oak with twisting branches and small, dark, shiny leaves, six of them. The black stallion, the foal, which I was now calling Dark Angel, and its mother. The younger sorrel stallion that looked a little like a palomino. And two other mares. I stood, catching my breath, watching. The air was still, and they twitched their ears and swished their long tails, shooing flies. They looked like a family, all grazing on this rugged land together. The stallion raised his head and looked at me. He seemed to be considering whether I was a threat. I stood still, angling my head away, not making eye contact, so I didn't look like a predator. I'd read in one of my horse books about relating to horses like that. He lowered his head again to graze.

Moving slowly, I sat down, took a swig of my water, and removed the baggie with the apples and carrots from my pocket.

I was dying to get closer and see if I could touch one of the horses, but I patiently sat and watched. The mustangs had a loose, rhythmic walk that I could watch all day. Just being around them made me feel relaxed. They were small, but their proportions were so perfect. I loved watching the pecking order in a herd, just like the pecking order in a group of kids at school. The black stallion was in charge of the group. The younger sorrel stallion was full of energy, circling a small bay mare, while Dark Angel followed her mother around like a shadow, wobbling on her skinny, knobbed legs, staying close to her mother's shoulder, her slanted, brown eyes never leaving her. The mother was caring in a tough sort of way, nuzzling Dark Angel and making sure she was always with her.

I slowly moved the slightest bit closer, imagining the joy of the moment I first touched one of them. The young sorrel stallion caught my attention. He was spirited, breaking into a canter, whirling, and throwing heel kicks. He circled behind the small bay mare, lowering his head and trying to herd her.

I loved his spirit. I named him Firecracker.

Just as I moved a bit closer, the black stallion trotted over to Firecracker, lowered his head, and tried to separate him from the mare. Firecracker trotted a few yards away and then wove his way back in the bay's direction. The stallion's ears snapped erect. He lowered his head and pawed the ground.

The other mares moved a slight distance away, the mother nudging the foal along. In a matter of seconds, I realized that I was now watching the two stallions, the black and the young sorrel, face off. The black stallion was reclaiming the bay mare.

Suddenly, with a screeching whinny, the black laid back his ears, rose on his hind legs, and lunged at the sorrel. Their bodies, as they collided, made a sickening thudding sound. Firecracker stumbled backward, then whirled and rose to his hind legs, kicking up clouds of sand, his teeth bared.

The two pawed, kicked, and twisted their heads, each trying to reach the other's jugular vein. The sounds were awful—the thud of their bodies colliding, their screams and grunts, the battering of their hooves on the ground. Swirling dust rose into the air. I held my breath, taking one step forward and then two back. At one point both of the black's front hooves rested on the sorrel's withers, just like they were dancing.

But they weren't. They were trying to kill each other.

The struggle continued, with high-pitched whinnies and sand exploding from their hooves, until at last the black sank his teeth into Firecracker's neck. Firecracker squealed in pain and wrenched himself away. Then the black raced back to the herd, pawing the ground, bucking, and tossing his head. Firecracker, after standing uncertainly for a moment, doggedly began to make his way back toward the herd, with his head lowered. The black wheeled and charged again, reared on his hind legs, and again aimed his teeth at the front of Firecracker's neck. Firecracker tried to pull away, but when the black's entire weight fell on him, his rear legs crumpled underneath. After a few long seconds, the black disentangled himself from Firecracker and galloped back to the herd. Firecracker dragged himself to his feet and trotted away, shaking his head as if to clear it.

Was the black kicking Firecracker out of the herd? I had read in my horse books that when one of the mare's colts became old enough, he sometimes would challenge the stallion who led the group. When this happened, whichever stallion loses the challenge would then be shunned from the group and be out on his own. Was Firecracker being shunned? I had read that the herd was everything to a wild horse. Wild horses knew that surviving without the safety of the herd was practically impossible. Would Firecracker survive? Would he find another herd?

Now the black was herding the mares and the foal away from Firecracker. He circled behind them, urging them toward a marshy area on the other side of the trees. I stared at Firecracker, holding my breath, as he stood looking longingly at the harem. Again he shook his head, and his straw colored mane feathered in the wind. He took a step toward the other horses, then pawed the ground with his small, neat hoof, and lowered his head again. My throat tightened and my eyes stung as I watched him.

Even though I never talked to anyone about it, I knew that feeling. I felt shunned at school. Like when people were talking about me behind my back, calling me "Animal."

Stephanie knew about my mood pills, but nobody else knew. Sometimes I worried that people would find out, but I was pretty sure she hadn't told.

Firecracker began to nibble at the sea grass a short distance from the herd, occasionally cocking one ear in the direction of the others. He took two steps toward them, then one step back.

I followed Firecracker, a little distance behind. Did he have a wound on his neck? Was he losing blood? What would happen to him? Would he battle his way back into the herd, or would he find another one?

He'd need strength. Now was the time to offer him the apples and carrots.

After an hour, I was sitting on a fallen log within ten feet of Firecracker. He was grazing along the side of the path, following the herd at a distance, never letting the rest of them out of his sight. I had finally gotten close enough to see that on the side of Firecracker's neck was a wound from the stallion's bite, and a thin stream of blood crawled through the fur on his neck toward his foreleg. Slowly, I got to my feet and held out half an apple at arm's length in the flat of my hand. I stood very still and talked to him.

"Are you doing okay? That's a good boy. How about

a nice, juicy apple. I promise I will never hurt you. Here."

Firecracker slowly raised his head and snorted softly. I held very still, so I wouldn't spook him. His nostrils quivered as he smelled the apple.

He looked at me with tired, wary eyes and cautiously stretched out his slim, damaged neck, his velvety lip beginning to wrinkle.

8

STEPHANIE

For a while, I sat on the beach by myself. The tide was out, and the beach was wide and flat, with a few other families sitting under umbrellas. I had set up my chair near a tide pool that had collected in a low spot on the beach, then went down and stuck my toes in it. I loved tide pools. The were usually warmer than the water, and sometimes I could see little critters digging into the sand on the bottom, sending tiny bubbles squiggling to the surface. It was like its own little world.

While I waited for Diana, my mind kept going over the last day of school before break, about the way one of the eighth grade football players had called her Annn-i-MAL while we were in the hall between classes. I didn't know if she heard him. I wanted to keep ignoring it. That would be the easiest thing to do. But maybe not the right thing. I mean, what would I say if I was to stand up for her? And it's not as if she wanted my help. She barely talked to me at school! I didn't want to think about it.

After a while I checked my phone; almost an hour had gone by. What was Diana doing? And suddenly I knew. She wasn't coming down at all. She'd skipped out on me—again. I bet anything she'd gone to find the horses.

I put down my book and stood up, turning to look back toward the long, empty, wooden walkway to our house. The triangular window reflected back at me, like a blank stare.

What if Daddy and Lynn got back early for some reason, and Diana wasn't back? What if she got in trouble? What should I do?

I could take one of our bikes and look for her, but based on where we went yesterday, a bike wouldn't make it through the soft sand on some of the roads behind the dunes.

I sat down, leaned my head back, and closed my eyes. The insides of my eyelids were red with the bright sun.

Well, Diana could just get in trouble, that's all. She was on her own. I shouldn't have to run after her. I hated it when Daddy got mad at us, but she obviously didn't care. What did she care about, except horses?

I opened my eyes and sat up, trying to put Diana out of my head. I went back to the tide pool, sat at the edge, and put my feet in, watching the tiny crabs dig into the wet sand. Sticking my hand in the water, I picked up a dark mound of sand and watched the crabs busily dig to escape me, their tiny, white cone shaped shells sliding out of view.

I saw a tiny figure far away down the beach moving closer. I saw the gray hoodie and the regular movement of Cody's thin, dark legs, and I could feel my heart beat faster, pumping in my collarbone.

Could I get him to stop and talk to me? I decided to practice some of my tumbling on the flat area of the beach right by the water.

I put my hands over my head and did a round off. Slow and easy to start off. Then another. Then a couple of back handsprings. One direction. Then another.

One of the things we had to do for our cheerleading routine this year was a standing back tuck, so I stood very still, arms to my sides, took a few breaths, and pulled one. Perfect.

I planned it so that just as Cody ran by, I linked together a round off, a back-handspring-back-tuck, and a lay out. A long, unbroken stream of me flying through the air, twisting, landing, and taking off again. I landed clean and solid on both feet. Slightly out of breath.

He stopped.

"Wow!" He wiped sweat from his face with the tail of his T-shirt, then leaned over, his hands on his knees, to catch his breath. "That was amazing!"

"Thanks!" I felt myself blush, so I looked away.

He walked in a slow circle, still catching his breath, hugging a towel around his neck.

His dark hair was amazingly shiny, and he had a fun kind of energy that I liked in a way I couldn't explain. "How far did you run today?" I wiggled my toes in the tide pool, then noticed he was staring at them. For some reason I felt kind of self-conscious, so I stopped.

"Three miles. My normal distance. Are you on the cheerleading squad at your school?"

"Yeah."

"That looks pretty hard."

"It does take a lot of practice."

"You're good!" His teeth flashed with the compliment, and I could feel my face getting hot again.

"I don't know." I looked away. "Just average on my cheer squad. I used to take gymnastics, which helps." We were quiet for a minute. Then I asked, "So what's your mom studying?"

"She's studying the trees in the maritime forest, the way they grow and adapt to the weather. She's classifying a bunch of them."

"What do you mean?"

"They twist and grow close together, and entwine, so they protect each other from the wind and the salt. The maritime forest is really important for the island. The roots of the trees keep the sand from eroding."

"So do you know the names of a bunch of trees?"

"Let's see. Yaupon. Live oak. Palmetto. Red cedar. Loblolly pine."

"Cool! I'd love to spend more time here. It's great you get to come here when your mom is doing research."

"Yeah. Where's your sister? Isn't her name Diana?" he asked.

I shrugged. "Stepsister. I don't know. Our parents went to play golf, and she was supposed to come out on the beach with me, but she hasn't shown up."

"Where do you think she is?"

"I think she might have gone to look for the wild horses back behind the dunes. You know, where the sand paths wind through the forest and marshland. I feel like I should go look for her. "

"We could take the ATV and go look for her."

"Um …" I stared at him. I'd never ridden an ATV. Daddy and Lynn probably wouldn't like it. But it would be a good way to look for her. Much faster than walking.

"I'm a fantastic driver."

Wow! Maybe Diana was right about him being arrogant.

"Really?" I ignored the thought that Daddy and Lynn would probably say no to riding the ATV if I asked them. I could just do it, and if they got mad, I'd tell them I was looking for Diana. Hopefully I'd find Diana before they got back, and they'd never know. And I was tired of being scared of everything. I wanted to hang out with Cody. "Well, if you don't go too fast …" I stood up, wiping sand off my hands.

"Great!" He rose to his feet and started up the beach. I went to follow him, but he waved me back. "No, wait here, and I'll bring the ATV down." He ran toward the dunes, joyously twirling the towel above his head. I put my T-shirt and shorts on over my bathing suit and wished I hadn't forgotten my flip-flops. I had no shoes to wear. I shoved my phone in the back pocket of my shorts. Minutes later I heard the roar of the motor, and Cody skidded up in a dust cloud, carrying helmets and goggles in his hand.

"Put these on."

I slid the helmet on, tightening the chin strap; then he showed me how to pull the goggles over it. The helmet felt heavy and awkward at first, and right away my scalp got itchy and started to sweat. I pointed to the path that ran beside our house and his. "We probably need to go back that way. Yesterday the horses were grazing in the shade near the trees."

"I'll take you along the beach a little first, just so you can see what it's like." With a broad smile, Cody slid forward and patted the seat behind him. "Climb on!"

I threw my leg over the wide, black leather seat, hot under the sun. I had thought I could sit on the back of the seat without holding on to him, but right away I realized I'd have to put my arms around his waist. He must have changed his shirt while picking up the ATV, because it was dry and clean. At first I felt modest and tried not to lean against him, but the minute we took off, with an exploding blast of the engine, my head jerked back and I locked my arms around him and plastered myself against his back, hanging on for dear life.

The wind screamed by, whipping my hair out behind me, and the engine roared in my ears, making them feel numb. Sand churned up by the front wheels pelted my feet and calves, and the wind buffeted our T-shirts, making them cling to us in front and billow out in back. "Whoaaeeee!" It escaped from inside me, bubbling up. I couldn't help it. The four-wheeler ate up the sand. Laughing, Cody drove down by the edge of the water and sprayed me, sending rainbows of water arcing behind us on both sides. I screamed, but I was laughing at the same time.

He veered away from the water.

The sky spread above us, brilliant and crisp, and the sand and water flashed by with amazing brightness on either side. I held my breath and grasped Cody's waist so tight I wondered if he could feel my heart pounding inside my chest. Thinking about that, I got kind of embarrassed, and goose bumps rose on my arms in spite of the heat.

"Watch this!" he yelled back at me as he veered farther away from the water and crossed onto the drier, more mounded sand. He drove the four-wheeler up one side of a dune, cresting the top, and then we were airborne! We flew a foot off the ground on the way down the other side, landing with a jolt and surging forward. I was so scared my cheeks were shaking. I buried my face in his shoulder.

Then he veered even farther from the flat sand and headed inland, along the path past our houses, past the dunes, and into the shadowed darkness of the maritime forest.

DIANA

A loud engine and then brakes sounded behind me, and a woman yelled, "Stop! You're breaking the law!"

At the sound of the words, Firecracker startled, tossing his beautiful head, and trotted away. After all the time I had spent getting close to him!

I whirled. Behind me, standing beside a small white SUV, was a wiry, tanned woman with gray hair in a bun, wearing khakis and hiking boots. And she looked mad.

"What?" I said, letting my empty hand drop to my side. Firecracker had already eaten the apple as well as all the carrots I'd brought.

"We have a county ordinance that says it's against the law to feed the wild horses," the woman said. "Haven't you seen the signs?"

"No," I said. Maybe there had been some signs, but I hadn't stopped to read them.

"They're only about eight feet tall," said the woman, raising her eyebrows meaningfully. "It's against the law to attempt to feed, ride, or come closer than fifty feet to any of our wild horses. Doing any of those things can get you arrested."

"Arrested?" I said, feeling the muscles in my chest tightening.

"Absolutely. The horses have their own special diet in the wild. They can get colic and possibly die if they eat things like carrots and apples like domestic horses," said the woman. "How would you feel if you knew that a horse had gotten colic and died from something you fed him? And you shouldn't get close to them because even though the horses see lots of people and aren't afraid of them, they're not tame, they're wild. They can kick or bite you."

"Firecracker wouldn't kick or bite me. I love horses, and I've been around them a lot. I've been riding and helping out at a barn for almost two years."

"Horses kick and bite even the most experienced trainers," said the woman with a patient smile.

I glared at her. "Who are you, anyway?"

"I'm Sally. I've been volunteering for the wild horse organization for many years. I check on them and make sure they're doing okay."

"I can see how you would need that ordinance for regular people, but I love the horses. I'm learning about horse whispering. I try to read their minds. I try to act like a horse. That ordinance shouldn't apply to someone like me."

"The ordinance applies to everyone," Sally said, almost gently.

I looked at the ground, searching for a change of subject. "While I was watching the herd, I saw Firecracker and the black stallion get into a fight. I think Firecracker has a bite on his neck."

"Oh, really?" Sally walked over closer to Firecracker to get a look at him. He was grazing now, more than fifty yards away, with the wound facing away from us. "So you named the sorrel stallion Firecracker?" Sally said. She looked at me steadily for a minute.

I was kind of embarrassed. "Yeah."

"You really care about the horses, don't you?" she said.

"Yes. Will Firecracker be okay?"

"I don't know. Stallions will fight. I'd been watching the black stallion and the sorrel and thinking it might happen soon."

"I think that's what just happened. The black stallion kicked him out. What will happen to him?"

"We'll see if the sorrel can find another harem, or maybe he'll join the herd of bachelor stallions."

"Bachelor stallions?"

"The stallions that are either too young or too old to have their own harems. Another possibility is that we'll have someone adopt him. We try not to interfere unless one of the stallions is so badly injured he can't take care of himself."

"How badly is Firecracker injured?"

"I'll have to keep an eye on him and see. But thanks for letting me know what you saw." Sally nodded to show her gratitude.

"So, are you going to have someone arrest me?" I demanded.

Sally looked at me steadily for a minute. "I'm just going to give you a warning this time, but make sure you remember how serious this is. And maybe, since you're such a horse lover, you can do your part to help out while you're here."

"What do you mean?" I said.

"If you see anyone getting too close, or trying to feed

or ride the wild horses, or being cruel to the horses in any way, let me know." She took a business card from her pocket and handed it to me. "The number for the Wild Horse Fund is on that card. Call and let us know what you've seen. And if you see that the sorrel seems to be so badly injured that he can't take care of himself, let them know about that too. These horses have it tough. They're losing their habitat, they're being shot at and poisoned. The mothers and foals especially are stressed by all the people around them. Some of the horses have been hit by cars and other vehicles. These horses are truly beleaguered. Imagine how you'd feel if you were losing your home. They need all the help they can get."

I looked at her card, then carefully slid it into the tiny pocket of my shorts. "Deal."

Sally sauntered over to watch Firecracker. "What's your name, young lady?"

"Diana."

"Are you staying around here?" she asked.

"A couple of miles away. I ran here."

"Do your parents know you're out here?"

"No."

"Be careful about staying out in the sun too long. You shouldn't be running without water."

"I hate to leave Firecracker." I focused on the way

his long tail swished as he grazed. "I feel so sorry for him, getting kicked out. He's all alone. Will he try to go back?"

"Maybe."

"But the black stallion won't let him come back?"

"Probably not. Nature is tough," Sally said. "Animals have to adjust to survive. He'll have to find another harem, somehow."

"How many horses are in the whole herd?" I asked.

"About a hundred and ten."

She explained that most people believe the horses came back in the early 1500s, when the Spanish conquistadores came to colonize the Outer Banks. "When their ships arrived in shallow water, sailors would sometimes push the livestock overboard and make them swim ashore," Sally said. "Sometimes ships would get stuck in the shallow water and break apart, and the horses swam ashore to safety. Other times, when the Spanish settlers died or the colony failed, they were unable to care for their livestock, and the horses began to forage for themselves and gradually became wild. By the 1800s there were hundreds of wild horses roaming the banks, and twice a year residents would round them up and pen and brand them. Many people tamed the horses to work on the farms or to help haul fishing nets. At one time there were thousands of wild mustangs on the Outer Banks. But a few years ago, when the Wild Horse Fund moved the horses up to Carova, there were only about sixty."

"Wow. What happened to them all?"

"Well, a lot of them were penned and tamed. In just the past decade, more than twenty of the mustangs have been shot."

"Shot?" I couldn't believe it. Who in the world would shoot a horse?

Sally nodded. "And as more people have begun to come here to live and vacation, sometimes they hit them and drive away without even reporting it."

"I can't believe someone would do that," I said.

Sally nodded again. "Now the Wild Horse Fund offers rewards to people who witness cruelty to the horses and report it so that those involved can be charged with crimes. We're also working on getting a law passed to protect the wild horses. They're a important legacy of the Outer Banks. For one thing, we need to keep people away from them."

What she meant was, other people. Not people like me.

"We are trying to grow the herd to prevent inbreeding. When they inbreed, they become more susceptible to disease and weakness.

"I saw a new foal in the harem with the black stallion. I named her Dark Angel."

"Yes, she's only a week old. This is foaling season, and we're excited because we've got a couple more foals coming along soon. During foaling season we have to be very careful that the mares and foals aren't stressed by the presence of too many people. The foals need time to nurse and bond with their mothers."

On the sandy road behind us, we saw a small chestnut stallion accompanied by a sorrel mare and a foal. As the stallion lowered his head to herd his family down the road, a bulldozer pulled out of a cul-de-sac, blocking the family's progress. The mare, confused, stopped, even though the stallion continued to try to herd her toward the bulldozer. Finally all three horses stopped, and the stallion, reconsidering, began to herd them in the opposite direction. Their heads hung low in the heat, their long manes stringy and matted with sweat.

"This is the story of their life," Sally said.

"Do they have to remove horses from the herd very often?" I asked.

"Not too long ago, a mare had to be taken out of the herd because of a trauma wound to her neck. After she got well, she wasn't able to return to the herd because she had been exposed to the diseases of domestic horses." Sally hesitated, then went on. "Sometimes the horses become too used to people. One of our horses a few years ago knocked a woman down trying to get her to feed him. So the herd manager had to remove him from the herd."

"And they can never go back?"

"No."

A lump formed in my throat, and tears pricked my eyes. It sounded so final. Why was nature so cruel?

"When they remove the horses from the herd, what do they do with them?"

"They adopt them out. The fund works with a couple of experienced horse trainers in particular to gentle the horses before they're adopted. We make a point of finding really good homes for these guys. So, I hope that sorrel can stay in the wild. But if he can't, we'll make sure he has a good home. I've got to be going." Sally climbed back into her SUV. "But if you see that the sorrel is looking worse—or if anyone is being cruel to the horses—get in touch."

"I will."

"Take care, Diana."

I waved as she pulled away.

I walked home. The broad sky arched over me, a pale, washed-out blue with a few tattered wisps of clouds. The water had looked choppy and green yesterday, but today it was calmer, and an iridescent shade of blue.

Just beyond the dunes, I saw the triangular window of our gray house. I recognized Stephanie's beach towel hanging over the armrest of a chair sitting on the beach. But I didn't see her anywhere.

I headed inside. I drank a big glass of milk and ate a peanut butter sandwich. I had a lot to think about. I hadn't admitted to Sally that Firecracker had already eaten several carrots and an apple that I had fed him. If what Sally said was true, what I had fed Firecracker could make him sick, could give him colic.

I ran my hands over my face. If I had made Firecracker sick, I would never forgive myself. I made a promise to check on him tomorrow, and every day we were here, to make sure he was okay.

From the bottom of the stairs, I called for Stephanie. No answer. I went upstairs, and she wasn't in the bedroom either. I headed back out onto the beach and saw her towel and book, abandoned on her beach chair. Her phone was gone, though.

Then I noticed tire tracks beside her chair.

I could not believe that she'd be out riding the ATV with Cody. She'd never get on an ATV! She was so scared of everything. But here were the tracks, and she was gone.

Slowly, at first, I started jogging along, following the ATV tracks. I was already tired from running before, and then walking, and right away I started getting these twinges in my right calf that sometimes meant I was about to get a cramp. The sting of a blister throbbed on my left heel from sand getting into my socks.

After about a half mile, the tracks led to a place where they went in a circle. Then they peeled off to the area behind the dunes. What had happened?

I kept following the tire tracks, over the dunes through the soft sand leading to the houses behind the dunes, and then down sandy paths farther away from the water and into the maritime forest. Because I was so tired, I stopped and walked through the forest for a while, listening to see if I could hear the sound of the ATV nearby.

This was probably hopeless. Cody and Stephanie were going much faster than I was, and I'd never catch up. I rounded a corner, and gnats swarmed my face.

I arrived at a fork where grass had grown over the path, and I couldn't see the tire tracks anymore. Which way had they gone? I walked back and forth, but separating out the tracks I'd been following from other tracks was now impossible.

I thought I recognized where I was from yesterday. Then I heard a motor. It definitely sounded like an ATV. I stood to the side of the path, waiting, hoping, as it got louder and louder.

10

STEPHANIE

Cody and I came flying around the corner, past a huge live oak, with me holding on to him for dear life, and there was Diana. Her face was white and sweaty.

Cody put on the brake, causing me to slide more tightly against his back, and squealed to a stop beside her.

"Oh my gosh, there you are!" I said. "We've been looking for you."

"I've been looking for *you*!" she said.

"You look awful. Are you okay?" Because she looked so wiped out, I decided not to mention the fact that she'd left without even telling me where she was going.

"Yeah, I'm fine," she said. "Maybe a little weak from running so much and not eating much."

"Get on, and we'll head back," said Cody, turning his head to indicate the back of the ATV.

"Is there room for all three of us?" Diana said.

"I'll scoot up." I moved closer to Cody, leaving a narrow strip of seat behind me. I was sitting up so close to him, I felt my face get hot. "Cody, can you scrunch up a little bit?"

"Not much." He inched forward, I moved up again, and Diana climbed on behind me, wrapping her arms around my waist. Her skin felt cold and clammy against mine.

"Stephanie, I can't believe you're riding this thing!"

"I can't either," I said with a laugh. I was wedged between the two of them, with barely room to breathe. "I don't think they're built for three people."

"They're not," Cody said. "Ready?"

"Go slow!" I said.

"I'll try." He put the ATV into gear and took off down a path to our right.

"Where are you going?" Diana yelled to Cody, leaning forward.

"Back to the beach," he yelled.

"This isn't the right way," she shouted. "We have to go the other way, to the left. That's the way I came in."

"No, the path goes in a wide circle," he shouted.

"This is wrong," she mumbled furiously, just next to my ear. Her arms tightened around me.

The path we were on did seem to be heading deeper into the shadows of the forest. The twisted branches of the trees closed in more tightly around us, and a damp coolness seeped into the air. Pine needles covered the path, muffling the sound of the engine. My heart began to thump, and I broke out in a sweat. Maybe Diana was right. Maybe we were lost.

"Cody, are you sure you know where we're going?" I asked.

Then suddenly the path opened up, and we saw, in the middle of nowhere, a line of small shops, a café, some outdoor restrooms painted in pastels, and a sandy playground with spotty clumps of grass. All completely deserted. Not a soul was anywhere to be seen.

"What is this place?" Cody said, slowing us to a crawl.

"It seems like a deserted town, or a movie set," I said.

"Told you it was the wrong way," Diana said with an impatient tone.

Cody turned off the motor. "Listen." We heard the thundering sound of many hoofbeats in the sand, and also other engines in the distance. Gradually, the engines increased in volume, coming closer.

In a few seconds, a herd of horses we hadn't seen before, white-eyed with manes and tails flying, raced into the open area from a path on the other side, their hooves pounding the sand, their necks dark with sweat beneath their manes. Cody hit the foot brake and put one foot on the ground. As soon as the horses saw us, they veered off in a different direction, sending clouds of dust swirling.

"What's going on?" Cody said.

My chest tightened.

Then we saw. Two guys on ATVs emerged from the woods on the path, their engines grinding at ear-splitting volume, and the minute they spotted the horses, they turned and went after them.

"They're chasing the horses!" Diana yelled.

As the riders flashed through the open area, we caught snatches of their laughter. They were both stocky and helmetless—the same two boys we'd seen yesterday, with the buzz cut and the curly, blond hair. They glanced at us as they drove by but didn't acknowledge us at all, and soon we were looking at billows of their dust.

"Go after them! Make them stop!" Diana said.

Before I could tell them to let me off, Cody gave the ATV gas with a flick of his wrist. With a jerk that snapped my head back, we tore after them. I closed my eyes and tightened my hold on his waist, pressing my cheek against his back. Diana's arms wrapped even more tightly around me. The ATV leaped forward, bumping over the dunes and picking up speed, and we closed the gap between us. My heart was beating so hard I could barely breathe. When our ATV was a few yards behind them, Diana yelled, "Stop chasing the horses!" But with the noise of the three vehicles, there was no way to hear.

The boys turned and glanced at us and then picked up their speed. They began to pull away, following the horses that had all raced out of sight to the left of a stand of live oaks, except two foals in the rear, struggling to keep up with their mothers.

Cody, with another flick of his wrist, upped our speed. "I'm going to cut them off," he yelled back at me, and headed out to the right of the oaks.

I buried my face on his shoulder. As we curved around the trees, we spotted the horses on the other side, racing for a flat, marshy area just beyond us. Cody cut behind them and kept going straight, and in the next second, the other two boys emerged from the opposite side. They veered to our right to try to get by us and stay with the horses, but Cody stayed on target, aiming right at them.

"Hey!" Curly shouted. "Watch out!"

Cody didn't flinch. He kept going, heading directly for them.

"Cody!" I screamed, burying my head in his back.

The others, at the last minute, slammed on their brakes and skidded, brakes squealing, throwing up chunks of black dirt.

"What are you doing?" Buzz Cut screamed.

Cody hit the brakes and turned the handlebars into a skid so quickly, Diana and I both went flying.

I landed in a heap on the sand, sliding along my side, but I had so much adrenaline, I hardly felt a thing. As I scrambled to my feet, Diana was already up, screaming at the boys, shaking her fist at them.

"How dare you! Stop it! Stop chasing the horses!"

"What's wrong with you? What the hell were you doing?" yelled Curly.

"She said don't chase the horses!" Cody said.

"Are you kidding?" said Buzz Cut. "Are you trying to kill us, you moron?"

"Stay out of our way, you stupid idiots!" yelled Curly.

When those words came out of their mouths, I felt like someone had just slapped me in the face.

"Shut up!" Diana shouted. "These horses are defenseless! They aren't hurting you! Leave them alone!"

"You shut up!" said Buzz Cut. "Come on, Jesse. Let's get outta here."

My chin had begun to tremble, and I was afraid I would cry if I tried to talk.

Curly revved his engine and spun away, deliberately trying to spray dirt in our faces. Buzz Cut lurched after him.

"I'm going to report you!" Diana choked out, running after them.

I was shaking all over.

"Stephanie, are you okay?" said Cody.

"I … I'm not sure." I looked down and saw I had scrapes and bruises on both legs, and one of my arms was bleeding. "I … I just feel like someone beat me up. What were you doing? We could have crashed."

Cody shrugged. "Diana said to go after them."

"Do you do everything people tell you to do?"

"Well, it worked," said Diana. She was trying to brush sand and dirt from a scrape on her thigh. One of her elbows was bleeding. But she was looking at Cody with a new, respectful expression on her thin face.

"Luckily!" I said.

"Are you okay, Diana?" Cody asked.

"Yeah."

"Whew." I sat down on the ground, just to stop the trembling of my legs. "Imagine how scared those horses must have been, with people chasing them like that."

"I'm going to report them," Diana said, wiping dirt from her cheek. "I met a lady who's a volunteer for the Wild Horse Fund. I'm going to call them and tell them what we saw."

"What lady?" I said.

"A lady named Sally. She told me to let them know if I saw anyone trying to feed or ride or hurt the horses." Diana straightened and squared her shoulders. "The horses are wild. This is where they live. They need to be protected from people."

"Weren't you saying yesterday that you wanted to feed and ride them?" I asked.

Since talking to Sally, Diana had changed a hundred and eighty degrees in the way she thought about the horses.

"Well, she explained some things to me," Diana said quickly. "Anyway," she said, changing the subject, "let's try to remember what those guys looked like."

"Let's see, that one guy had blond, curly hair." I described them as well as I could. "He had on a red T-shirt and jeans. The other had a buzz cut. One earring and a white T-shirt. Both of them were kind of heavyset."

"The blond one was driving a black Yamaha Raptor," Cody said. "The other guy drove an old red Mongoose, just like this one."

"Oh, good!" Diana said with admiration. "I was looking at the guys, not the four-wheelers."

Diana pulled a business card from her pocket. "Can I borrow a cell phone?" I handed her mine, and she punched in the number, listened for a minute, then mouthed to us, "Answering machine." After a moment she said, "I just wanted to report that I was in the maritime forest behind the dunes and saw two boys on ATVs chasing some of the wild horses." She then carefully described the boys as well as the ATVs and then hung up.

The names the boys had called us flashed through my mind again. And once again, Diana and Cody had been brave and stood up to them, while all I could do was try not to cry and crouch out of sight.

My phone dinged with a text message, and I opened it. "Oh my gosh." I stared at Diana. "Daddy and Lynn are on their way home."

11

DIANA

"We're going to get in so much trouble," Stephanie said, and I swear she was about to cry. I wanted to smack her and say, "Snap out of it!"

"Okay, we'll head back, but we'll get Cody to let us off before we get to our house so they'll think we went for a walk on the beach," I said.

"But what about our scrapes and bruises?" Stephanie said, rubbing blood from her arm.

Cody picked up his helmet and shook out the sand. "So your parents wouldn't want you to ride the ATV?"

"I don't want to ride again," Stephanie said. "I'll walk back."

"That'll take too long," I said.

So, after a second, Stephanie climbed on behind Cody, and he scooted way up on the seat so I could get on the back. Stephanie put her arms around Cody's waist again, and I put my arms around hers, while my feet dangled beside the big cratered wheels.

"Ready?" Cody turned the key and hit the start button. The engine fired to life.

"Go slow!" Stephanie shouted.

"I am!" he yelled over the engine. He put it in gear, and we headed down the sun-dappled path as it wound through the trees, the wide wheels rolling ever so sedately over the pine needles and sand. In the warmth of the sun, I could smell the apple shampoo in Stephanie's hair and the coconut of her suntan lotion. Cody probably could too. On the other hand, I'm pretty sure I smelled like sweat.

We meandered slowly along through the forest, the sound of the four-wheeler muffled by the pine needles. None of us spoke until we made it back out onto the beach.

I told Cody to stop and let us off, then jumped off the back.

"Whew," said Stephanie, slowly crawling off the vehicle.

Stephanie lightly touched Cody's arm as she handed him back her helmet. Unbelievable. She really did it to me sometimes.

"You're both okay?" Cody snapped the helmet under the seat.

"Yeah." I looked at Stephanie's scrapes and my own. "Let's wash off in the ocean."

So as Cody roared off, we went down to the water's edge and splashed the ice cold water over our arms and legs to get the sand and dirt and blood off. Stephanie squealed every time the water touched her skin. The scrape below her elbow was pretty bad. I had a huge bruise on my hip, but you couldn't see it because of my shorts.

"Let me do the talking," I said to her as we started walking back. "Here's our story: We just went for a walk on the beach and had trouble remembering which one our house was. Cover that scrape with a towel as soon as you get there."

"I'm not a good liar."

"I know. You're terrible. That's why I said I'd do the talking."

Stephanie didn't respond, and we walked along silently for a few minutes.

"So when you went to look for the horses, why didn't you at least come tell me what you were doing?" she finally asked.

I scuffed my toes on the sand. "I figured you'd try to talk me out of it."

She nodded, and we walked in silence for a little bit longer. We passed a large sign on a post beside a dune, and I realized this was one of the warning signs that Sally had been referring to. In large letters, it said not to feed, ride, or come within fifty feet of the horses.

Stephanie examined the scrape on her elbow, which was still bleeding a little.

"So," I said, "how did Cody ever convince you to ride the four-wheeler? I never would have thought you'd do that in a million years."

"I know!" she said. Her eyes got wide, and she smiled. "Me neither. He hardly said anything really. I just got fed up with being scared."

"I can't believe you rode with him." It seemed like Stephanie had a split personality that shifted when there was a boy around.

"He's nice," Stephanie said and then smiled. "And cute. Don't you like the way he pushes his glasses up on his nose—so studious."

"You think every boy is cute," I said.

"That's not true at all!" Stephanie checked her elbow again. She wiped some blood away.

In the distance we spotted Mom, still wearing her golf clothes and visor, standing beside Stephanie's beach chair, with her hands on her hips, staring down the beach at us.

"Uh-oh," Stephanie said. "She probably saw Cody drive by already. She might think we were together. Maybe we should have waited longer."

"Just follow my lead," I said.

When we got within about fifty feet, Mom hurried toward us. "Where have you been?" She crossed her arms tightly over her chest, cocking her head at us.

"Just for a long walk on the beach," I said. "You didn't want us to stay here the whole time you were gone, did you?"

"No—but you should have left a note." She joined us walking back toward the chair.

"Oh my gosh, I'm sorry!" Stephanie exclaimed. "We forgot!" I glared at her. She was acting way too sorry. She caught my eye and bit her lip, then grabbed the towel from the chair and awkwardly draped it over her arm. She might as well have had a neon sign on her forehead that said, "I fell off the ATV and scraped my arm." Ugh. She was hopeless.

"I just saw that boy Cody drive by on his four-wheeler a few minutes ago," Mom said. "He went flying over a dune. Those things are so dangerous."

I tagged along behind Mom and Stephanie on the walkway, listening to Mom's inevitable list of physician's assistant stories from the trenches. Just two weeks ago a teenager had fallen off an ATV and required thirty-six stitches in her forehead. Just last week a teenager broke his ankle in an ATV crash. Last year three teenagers wrecked an ATV and were killed. I touched Stephanie on the shoulder, and when she glanced around, I rolled my eyes and did a talk-talk-talky motion with my fingers. She smiled weakly and looked away.

Suddenly Mom looked at the towel draped over Stephanie's arm. "Stephanie, there's blood on that towel. Are you hurt?"

"No, it's okay." Stephanie tried to hide her arm, but Mom peeled back the towel and examined the scrape.

"She was doing some cheerleading stuff and tripped over a piece of driftwood that was out on the beach," I said. I looked at my throbbing leg and saw the bruise was spreading down my thigh, so I grabbed a towel and put it around my waist so Mom wouldn't see.

Stephanie looked at me wide-eyed as we headed through the back sliding door of the cottage into the living area.

"Oh, honey, that's a bad scrape. You should be careful with that tumbling on the beach. Diana, while I wash Stephanie's arm, will you please go get the first-aid kit from under the sink in our bathroom? And get some bandages out for me."

"Sure." I got the kit and started taking out some bandages when Mom's cell phone started ringing.

"Diana, could you pick that up?" Mom said.

I delivered the kit and grabbed her phone. "Hello?"

There was a brief silence on the other end, and then I heard an enthusiastic "Oh, hey there, dudette!"

That was a nickname he'd started using for me lately. It was Dad.

My heart squeezed and turned a flip.

"How's the vacation going?" he said. "You guys having lots of fun?"

"Yeah, so far."

"Good, good." It sounded like he was flipping through papers. Multitasking again, only focusing part of his brain on the conversation. Sometimes he used his salesman's voice with me. "My conference is going well too."

"When will we get together?" Suddenly I felt dizzy. Dad's voice sounded faint, and I started seeing black spots dance before my eyes. I remembered I hadn't eaten yet. And maybe I'd run too far.

"Later this week, we'll definitely get together. I have somewhere I want to take you."

"Where?" My throat went dry. I definitely needed a drink.

"It's a surprise! It's going to be very cool. Hey, maybe I better talk to your mom to arrange the details."

I glanced over at Mom. She was putting the finishing touches on the gauze she'd wrapped around Stephanie's forearm. "Just a minute," she said, giving Stephanie a tight smile, then patting her shoulder. Mom took the phone from me, playing nervously with her earring. "Hello, Steven."

12

STEPHANIE

When Lynn took the phone, I glanced at Diana to see what happened next. She raised her eyebrows and barely shook her head, like she was saying, *Don't know, but there's nothing we can do now.*

I couldn't believe Diana lied so easily to Lynn. And soon Daddy would come in from cleaning the golf clubs, and we'd lie to him too.

While Lynn talked on the phone with Diana's dad, Diana watched her like a dog eyeing steak on a plate.

"She can come and spend the day with you, but we'll pick her up before dinner," Lynn said in a real firm voice. I went and stood right at the front door so I could hear the conversation but also see what Daddy was doing. Daddy, still out behind the car, was reorganizing his golf bag. Clubs lay crisscrossed on the sand, along with a stack of little white balls, bags of tees, and a couple of golf gloves. Cody stood there talking to him, and Daddy handed him a club. Cody practiced swinging it. It looked like Daddy gave him some tips, because Cody swung the club again. Daddy nodded and smiled. Cody handed back the club and headed toward his house.

It looked like Cody had made friends with Daddy, which was great. It made me feel a little guilty, because if Daddy knew we'd been riding on the ATV and fell off, he might not let us hang out with him anymore.

Lynn, still wearing her goofy golf visor, paced around the couch while she talked to Diana's dad. "You're not going to take her parasailing or anything crazy like that, are you? We've already got our hands full this week." Lynn listened for a minute. "All right," she said. "We'll meet you at the entrance to Jockey's Ridge at ten-thirty Thursday morning. And Steven ... please call if you're going to be late." She closed the phone, leaned over the counter, pulled off her visor, and ran both hands through her hair.

And then Daddy walked in. "Hey, that Cody is a nice young man. I told him that we're going to the aquarium and the Wright Brothers Memorial tomorrow and invited him to come along with us. That okay with everybody?"

"Sure!" I said.

Lynn nodded. "Sure, that sounds fine. And then the next day Diana is going to visit her dad. I just talked to him."

"That go okay?" Daddy asked, focusing on Lynn.

"Yeah."

"Diana, your mom hit some great shots today," Daddy said. "She beat me on two holes, can you believe that? So, how did you say you did this to your arm, Stephanie?" Daddy asked, touching the bandage Lynn had made.

I hesitated. Diana had lied just now, to Lynn. But I couldn't do it. I knew Diana was expecting me to do it, and I couldn't even look in her direction. I felt the blood pounding in my neck. "We ... uh ... fell off the ATV."

Daddy took off his golf hat, scratched his head, and looked at me. "You did what?"

I could feel Diana's furious eyes on me, the freckles standing out on her white face. "Stephanie!"

I drew a deep breath. "We were riding the ATV too fast and fell off."

"How did you end up doing that?" Lynn said, with confusion in her voice.

I went over to the couch and sat down. "Well … Diana went out for a run, and she was gone a long time and I got worried, so I asked Cody to give me a ride on the ATV to look for her. And then we found her, and we were riding back—"

"The three of you?" Daddy said.

"Yes, and we saw some guys on ATVs chasing the wild horses, and we went after them to make them stop. And that's when we fell off."

"Diana you lied to me! Are *you* hurt?" Lynn asked.

"Just some bruises," Diana mumbled.

"So the three of you rode on the ATV?" Daddy said. He had his hands on his hips, his eyebrows had swooped downward, and his mouth was a straight line.

Diana stared at him unblinkingly, without answering, crossing her arms over her chest.

"Lynn, you want to talk about this in the bedroom for a minute?" Daddy asked.

"Sure."

"Diana, have a seat on the couch with Stephanie," Daddy said. "We'll be back in a minute."

Daddy and Lynn went into the bedroom. The door clicked shut behind them.

I pulled my feet up and sat cross-legged. My arm started to throb. Diana sat down next to me, glaring.

"I can't believe you told," she hissed, her eyes dark with anger.

From behind the door, we heard the low rumble of their voices.

"I'm sorry."

"You're so lame."

I heard Lynn's voice rise, and then Daddy's. Then Lynn's again. The doorknob turned, but the talking continued, and the knob turned back.

Finally the bedroom door opened, and Daddy and Lynn came out and sat down on the love seat across from us. "Lynn and I have discussed this," Daddy said, "and we agree that it makes no sense for you two to be grounded while on vacation. It would ruin the vacation for the whole family. So you'll be grounded for a week when we get back."

"And that's grounded from everything, including your cell phones and the computer," Lynn added.

"I don't have a cell phone," Diana said.

"When I think about all the things that could have happened ..." Daddy kept on talking about the dangers of riding with so many people on an ATV, and I couldn't help thinking about Cody. Did he get hurt at all? Would he offer a ride to me again?

"What I just don't understand," Daddy was finally saying, "is why would you do this?"

"I was worried about Diana," I said quickly. I looked at Daddy's face. He looked so upset and concerned. I would never tell him I thought Cody was cute, and I didn't want him to know how afraid I was. Out of the corner of my eye, I could see Diana's stiff profile. She was probably worried I was going to tell that she never came down to the beach, but I'd never do that. "It was bad judgment," I added. "But it won't happen again."

"Well, no, it certainly won't. That four-wheeler is off-limits from now on."

"What about Cody? Can he still go with us tomorrow?" I asked.

Daddy stopped talking and sat back, crossing his arms to look at us. I saw understanding dawn on Lynn's face. Now they realized that I liked Cody. With that one question, I'd given everything away. Ugh.

"Well … it's obvious he doesn't have good judgment," Daddy said, gesturing impatiently with his arm and glaring at Lynn. "But neither do our girls. Why is it that when the two of you are together, we always run into problems?"

"We can hardly uninvite him for tomorrow, Norm," Lynn said.

Suddenly there was a soft knock on the front door. Lynn, startled, jumped up and crossed the room. When she opened the door, Cody stood there with a woman who must have been his mother, since she looked amazingly like him. She was vivacious and tanned with short, dark hair.

"Hello," Lynn said, opening the door wide and stepping back to let them in. "Please come in."

"Hi there! I'm Malia Clark, and I guess you met Cody. " Mrs. Clark shook hands with Lynn and Dad. You could tell she spent a lot of time outside in the sun and hiked a lot.

"Cody tells me there was an accident on the ATV this afternoon," said Mrs. Clark, coming over toward me. "How are you doing, honey?"

"I'm okay," I said. I tried to catch Cody's eye, but he wouldn't look at me. He came in my direction, though. I thought he might sit next to me on the couch, but instead he sat on the armrest.

"We're so sorry this happened," said Mrs. Clark as soon as everyone had gotten settled. She looked at Lynn. "She doesn't need to go to the emergency room, does she?"

"No, she's okay," Lynn said. "Her arm is scraped, but it will be fine. It's nice of you to come over and check."

"I was really worried when Cody told me what happened," said Mrs. Clark. "And I wanted to make sure everything was all right. The ATV belongs to the owners of our rental house," she added. "Cody didn't know that two people aren't supposed to ride on them."

"I'm sorry," Cody said. "If there are medical expenses, I'll pay."

With that, Lynn's shoulders relaxed, and she let out a sigh. "Accidents happen," she said with a smile. "Are you still planning on coming with us tomorrow, Cody?"

Cody glanced at Mrs. Clark, who nodded. "Sure, if it still works for you, that would be great. I'm out working on my research quite a bit, and he gets left on his own."

"What kind of research do you do?" Lynn asked.

"I'm trying to record all of the types of trees in the maritime forest here. I was here last summer, and I'm trying to finish up my report by the end of this semester."

"That sounds fascinating," Daddy said. His tone sounded gentler too.

"I love it! The forest is a never-ending source of wonder. And most people don't realize how important the maritime forests are to the ecosystem. I can't spend enough hours of the day working on this … Isn't that right, Cody?"

Cody grinned. "She's pretty obsessed."

Mrs. Clark stood up, and so did Cody. "Anyway, thanks for inviting him for tomorrow. He's really anxious to see the aquarium. ."

"Thanks for coming by," Norm said. "We'll send one of the girls over tomorrow morning when we're ready to leave."

As they left, Cody finally turned a shy smile on me and gave a slight wave. "Later," he said.

"That was nice of them to come over, wasn't it?" Lynn went into the kitchen, turned on the fluorescent light, and started getting out the dishes. "She seems like a very together person, doesn't she?"

I went upstairs and lay down on my stomach on my bed. Afternoon sun angled in bright stripes across the porch.

Diana came and stood in the doorway. "Thanks for getting me grounded."

"Sorry," I said. "But they would have found out when Cody and his mom came over anyway." I put my pillow against the wall and sat up against it. "Next week seems so far away anyway. "

After a second, Diana came in, closed the door, and proceeded to sit cross-legged on my bed. "Everywhere you go, you find some boy in, like, ten minutes." Her voice had a jealous tone.

"I do not," I said and felt my face reddening.

"Yes, you do."

"Well, I like being friends with boys." I went to the dresser and started brushing my hair.

"Duh." She played with the fringe of her cutoffs, not looking at me "So have you ever had a boyfriend?"

I thought a minute, pulling my hair up into a ponytail. "No, but my friend Colleen was with a guy most of last summer. They were together all the time. He ate dinner at her house with her family. They texted each other constantly. I couldn't even have a conversation with her because of the texting. She didn't want to go to the pool or shopping or hardly anything. They were obsessed with each other."

"That sounds annoying."

"Then all of a sudden he broke up with her, like, out of the blue. She was devastated. Then he went out with some other girl for three weeks and then broke up with her. But it's okay, because now Colleen likes someone else."

"See? It sounds horrible."

"Do you really think boys are horrible," I asked, then something occurred to me. "Or are you just scared of them." Could Diana-the-fearless be afraid of something after all?

I sat down on the bed next to her. "I can't really explain it," I said before Diana could answer. "I think boys are funny. I love kidding around with them, but I think a lot of guys our age are still more interested in video games. I mean, Matt is eighteen and has a girlfriend, but he acts like he would rather shut him-self in the basement with his Xbox than be with her." I glanced at Diana's bunched-up face, wondering if I could tell her about what Matt and his friends did. In the basement, before Mama got home from her job at the tennis club. They did all kinds of stuff. Sold Adder-all pills. Stole beer from someone's garage. I pictured Matt's furious face when he told me, "You better not tell anyone." So I hadn't.

"I don't trust boys," Diana said sharply, looking at her lap again. And my chance to talk about it was gone.

"What about Russell from the ranch last summer? You got to be friends. Did you guys ever talk to each other again?"

Diana shook her head. "No. I wrote him a letter, but he never wrote back. I think he was still mad at me for what happened to the wolves."

"Well, they found both of the wolves, so he should be cool with you now," I said.

"Apparently not."

I didn't really know what to say to that. "Well, if he's going to hold a grudge, then you don't need him. You, I mean *we* were just trying to help."

I thought about all that had happened. We were both silent. Russell had loved the wolves, Waya and Oginali, and he'd blamed Diana and me for what happened to them. We'd found Waya, and she'd been sent to a wolf rescue operation. Later, Oginali had been found too, and she was now at the same wolf rescue operation. Waya and Oginali were reunited. Ever since then we'd been sending most of our allowance to the Wolf Rescue Operation to help pay for their care. The wildlife workers had sent us some photos showing how healthy Waya and Oginali were now. Their searing yellow eyes were clear, and their gray and black coats were full and shiny.

"Have you and Nick talked?" Diana asked.

"We played his team in soccer last fall, and I saw him after the game. He has a girlfriend now. We're just friends. We text sometimes." Nick and I had fun hanging out while we were at the ranch, but I had a lot of other friends at home, and he did too. The truth was that Russell and Diana had more of a serious connection than Nick and I did. I put down my brush and picked up some wine colored nail polish and shook it, hearing the click of the tiny balls inside mixing the polish. "Maybe you not trusting guys has to do with your dad. Maybe you should give people more of a chance."

"Why do you keep saying that?" Diana said with sudden anger. "Maybe people should give *me* more of a chance."

"I'm sorry. I only meant—" I started to say.

"Maybe my dad should give me more of a chance!" Diana snapped. "Not everything is my fault!"

"Well, you're going to see him in two days. I hope it's great."

Diana heaved a deep sigh. She propped one pillow against the wall and stretched out her skinny legs along the other side of my bed. "He said he has a surprise for me. Wonder what it is!"

"Yeah?" I raised my eyebrows and smiled in my most excited way, but then looked down at the bedspread and played with a loose string.

"Anyway, guess what?" she said, lowering her voice. "I found an injured young stallion when I went out for a run. I'm going to sneak out tonight and go look for him."

I let my mouth fall open. "We're already grounded! You're going to get in a ton of trouble, Diana!"

"Not if you don't tell on me." She cut her eyes over at me.

"Diana, after all that happened last summer, I can't believe you would even think I'd tell!" I glared into her stubborn eyes. Last summer when she'd sneaked out, I'd even gone with her. But now we were already in trouble. I didn't want to do that again.

"Because you just told on us! You told that we fell off the ATV!"

"But Cody's mom came over—and if I hadn't told, we would have been in even more trouble!"

At that very moment Lynn knocked on the door of my room before poking her head in. "Hey! What's going on up here?"

"Nothing," Diana and I both said. *Had she heard our conversation?*

"I *love* seeing the two of you having girl talk," Lynn said, leaning against the doorjamb, with gentle eyes and a smile. So maybe she hadn't heard anything. Or maybe she just wasn't letting on.

13

DIANA

I woke up in the dark, and the sound of the waves surrounded me. I had no idea what time it was. I put on my running shoes, shorts, and a sweatshirt. Inch by inch, so quietly it did not make a sound, I pushed open the sliding door of my room and stepped out onto the porch. The moon, almost full, shone like a round, white shell high overhead, with ghostly clouds trailing in front of it like veils. A throbbing chorus rose from the night insects in the sea grass. Careful to avoid splinters, I climbed over the wooden railing and shimmied down the corner column until I could stand on the railing of the first floor porch just below. I lowered myself down to the porch itself, ran under the house, and then got my bike. I listened to the quiet *click-click* of the wheels as I rolled it down the long walkway to the water, shining like fractured silver in the moonlight.

The moon made it seem almost as bright as day.

And there, sitting on the beach, was a dark figure with a bent head. I gasped and stared for a minute, until I got closer and saw that the person was wearing a sleeveless hoodie.

What was he doing down here?

I tried to sneak by without talking to him, but the clicking of my bike wheels made him turn his head. "Hey, Diana."

I walked my bike over and asked him the question. "What are you doing down here?"

He shrugged and stood up, knocking sand from his shorts. His eyes glinted in the darkness. "I couldn't sleep, so I came out to see if there was any bioluminescence out here. There are creatures called noctilucae that sometimes glow blue."

"Noctilucae?" I scanned the ocean but didn't see any glow of blue. I hadn't liked Cody at all at first.

I had thought he was arrogant, talking about how I wouldn't understand the concept of bioluminescence. But I'd liked him trying to chase down those guys on the ATVs. And Stephanie had told me I needed to give people second chances. Maybe she was right.

"Have you seen anything?"

He shook his head and pointed at my bike. "Where are you going?"

"What time is it?" I asked, instead of answering his question.

He pulled his cell phone from his pocket and glanced at the cover. "Five–thirty."

Should I tell him? Stephanie and Dr. Shrink both told me I needed to trust people more. I thought about the connection I'd felt with Russell last summer, when we'd talked and admitted things. "I found a young stallion that was injured by another horse, and I wanted to see if I could find him and make sure he was okay."

"An injured wild horse?"

"Yeah."

"I'll come with you," he said, adjusting his glasses. The moonlight caught one of the lenses, turning it opaque, and the tips of his dark, curly hair.

"No, that's okay," I said quickly. I didn't want him coming with me. I felt stupidly out of breath and gave my head a shake, trying to clear it. I put one leg over my bike.

"Come on, there's nothing happening here, and I'm wide awake."

"No." I pushed down on the bike pedal, needing to get going.

"Does Stephanie have a bike? Could I ride it?" he persisted.

I glared at him.

Ten minutes later the waves roared in my ears and the wheels of Stephanie's bike whirred furiously beside me in the bright moonlight. The cool, damp, night breeze off the ocean raised goose bumps on my arms. Cody at least wasn't annoying me by trying to talk while we were riding, which Stephanie always did.

We rode by the roped off turtle nest and kept on going. I was acutely aware of him riding beside me, of the way his knees, when he pedaled, went up a bit too high, since Stephanie's bike was too small for him. Most guys wouldn't be caught dead on a girl's bike, but Cody didn't seem to care.

I was looking for the forked piece of driftwood, but before we got there, I noticed some odd looking, dark mounds on the beach. They looked like they were moving.

"What's that?" I called to Cody. We pedaled closer.

Something was definitely moving. As we moved toward it, I heard a low, terrible moan, like a child in pain, like something alive that was in pain. This sound was so wrenching, tears came to my eyes and my heart began to beat wildly. What could it be?

I rode closer, then let my bike drop in the sand. It wasn't Firecracker. It was the mare I had seen on the first day, lying on her side, moaning, snorting, and struggling to stand. And her black foal, Dark Angel, was beside her, its head down, nuzzling its mother, and whinnying softly.

I took a few steps closer, and Dark Angel lunged a few yards away from me, then stood trembling on her knobby legs, and crying almost like a goat.

I watched the mare flail and saw that she wasn't able to use one of her hind legs. A thin sliver of the white of her eye flashed as she jerked her head in the moonlight. "It's her leg."

"What can we do?" asked Cody. He was right behind me.

My mouth was completely dry. The mare's moans made me feel sick to my stomach, and a cold sweat broke out on my arms and neck. I couldn't stand to see animals in pain. Last summer when I'd found Waya, the wolf, and she'd been shot, I had almost fainted.

I wanted to go to the mare, touch her, stroke her, and

soothe her. But she was wild. Touching her wouldn't soothe her. It would only scare her.

I took some deep breaths. Tried to calm the wall of panic in my brain.

If we called anyone, we'd get in trouble for being out here. But we had to. We had to get help for her. Could we call without giving our names?

"Let me see your cell phone," I said to Cody. Silently he handed it to me, and with shaking fingers I punched in 911.

"Sheriff's department," said a man's clipped voice.

"Yes," I said, trying to control my breathing. "Out on the beach—where you drive on the beach—there's a wild horse that's lying on its side and can't get up. Someone might have hit it. And there's a foal too."

"Where are you?"

"On the four-wheeler part of the beach."

"What mile marker? There are green signs by the dunes. Can you find one near you?"

"Run up and find out what that mile-marker sign says!" I hissed at Cody.

He ran toward the nearest green sign and yelled it out to me. I gave the man the mile marker.

"Can I get your name, please?"

I took a breath. I couldn't do that. Without answering I hung up. We should leave now if we didn't want to get into trouble.

But how could I leave the mare and Dark Angel? She had tired of trying to get up and was lying on her side now, breathing heavily, her eyes wide and terrified. Her fur was streaked with sweat. Dark Angel, still afraid of us, had not come any closer but continued to whinny. She kept her mother between herself and us.

"Let's wait with her for a little while and then go hide in the sea grass when they get here," I said.

We sat down on the sand a short distance from the mare. Her side rose and fell with each painful breath. Just listening made me shaky and teary. Dark Angel lay down next to its mother and put its head on her flank.

A bright band glowed on the eastern horizon, and the sky lightened. A breeze blew off the ocean, some dried grass tumbled by, and I noticed a sand crab scuttle over tire tracks near the mare.

"Cody, look. Tire tracks."

"Really?"

"That's what it looks like. So someone hit her and then drove away!" Her streaked flank rose and fell, and the sound of her panting eclipsed the crash of the nearby waves.

"Wow," Cody said.

"I know! She seems weak now." What if she died? What would happen to Dark Angel? "I bet those kids we saw yesterday had something to do with this!" I said.

"You think?" he said.

The mare moaned suddenly and struggled again to get up. When the foal raised its head, its little anvil-shaped head, and nuzzled its mother, I scrubbed the tears off my cheeks. "Why would someone hit a mare with a baby foal?"

"I don't know," Cody said. "Maybe it was an accident."

I stood up, barely able to take my eyes away from the mare and her foal. The sounds of the mare's suffering were burned into my memory forever and kept making me cry. I hated crying in front of Cody. I never cried in front of anyone!

"Someone will be here soon. We should hide or leave so we won't get in trouble," Cody said. We righted our bikes and walked them behind the first dune and crouched in the sea grass. Both of us sat hunched and cross-legged, listening to the mare.

Even though we'd only waited ten minutes, I got anxious.

"When is someone going to get here?" Cody said. "Maybe we should just leave."

A faint band of early morning sun filtered through the waving sea grass.

Cody hadn't said anything about me crying. He'd pretended not to notice. I was grateful he hadn't made fun of me, and I was starting to see why Stephanie liked him. One thing I had noticed about Stephanie was that she always saw the good in people. I had been in the habit, for a long time, of seeing only the bad.

And Cody's smile made a kind of tingle travel up my spine.

Only a minute or so later, two sets of headlights headed up the beach. They slowed as they approached the mare, and once again she tried to stand, moaning with the effort. A white SUV stopped, and two men jumped out. One had a beard, and the other had a gray ponytail and wore a baseball cap. An officer climbed out of the sheriff's car.

"It's Isabel and her foal!" said the man with the beard. "Someone has hit her."

The man with the baseball cap took a few steps toward the mare. "I would have to examine her. Let's use the darts so we can get close."

I realized the man with the baseball cap was a veterinarian. From the back of the pickup truck, he pulled out something that looked like a slim rifle and inserted a brightly colored dart. I was familiar with these from helping the vet with the wolves last summer. He took aim at the mare's haunch and fired.

Even though I knew the vet wasn't shooting her, that he was just sedating her, I still felt my throat tighten.

The dart took literally thirty seconds to work, and

she laid her head on the sand. The vet was able to approach her. The foal stumbled a short distance away and stood there bleating. The vet knelt and examined the mare's leg and flank, murmuring soft and soothing nonsense words.

As the sky began to lighten even more, he stood and talked with the other man, and they crossed their arms over their chests, nodding soberly. They glanced at the foal, then back at the mother.

What would happen to them? Thoughts whirled and buzzed in my head. I knew Cody and I should leave, but I couldn't tear my eyes away from the scene before me. I had heard many times at the barn that usually if horses broke their legs, they were put down. Would that happen to the mare? *Oh, please, please, don't let her die.*

Meanwhile, the officer had started to pace out the tire tracks on the beach. His hair was so short he almost looked bald, and he definitely looked like he worked out. He began to snap pictures of the tread marks, from different angles, then took out a measuring tape and measured the width of the tracks.

"Based on the size of these, I'd say we're looking for an ATV," he said to the other men. "And there's most likely some damage to the vehicle."

"Big surprise," said the man with the beard. "Kids."

"Look," said the officer. "There are some bicycle marks around here too."

I caught my breath and glanced at Cody.

"We can offer a reward, like last time," the officer said.

"Thanks," said the man with the beard.

"And I'll see what the trace on the 911 call turns up." He shook hands with the other men. "Good luck. I hate to see things like this. Sorry."

As the sheriff's car pulled away and headed back down the beach, a glow spread along the horizon. It was almost daylight.

"We need to leave," Cody said.

I nodded, roughly wiping my hair and the tears from my face, and we picked up our bikes. Before returning to the beach, we walked our bikes through the dunes for almost the length of a football field so the men wouldn't see us.

I hated leaving the mare lying there, but we had at least gotten help. As I pedaled down the beach, I whispered over and over, "Please let them save her." I remembered Stephanie asking me if I believed in God. I had said no. But who else would I be talking to if not to God?

Cody and I rode down the beach together, in a gray morning world, as a damp breeze from the ocean blew away scraps of the calls of the seagulls flying overhead. I was hoping we could get home before anyone missed us. Our bike tires made a grainy sound against the damp sand, like an old record at the end of the song. Gradually, faint streaks of pale purple shot through the sky and frosted the water. My eyes burned from lack of sleep. We found the wooden walkway to the house and walked the bikes along it as quietly as possible. My heart was pounding hard, and I was hoping Mom and Norm were still asleep and not looking out through the sliding door and seeing us. Cody didn't try to talk, and I was glad. We put the bikes back where we had found them.

"How can we find out what happens?" Cody asked quietly.

"We have to call later."

We had witnessed something horrible together. I hadn't cried in front of anyone in a long time. Even though I hated boys, I felt like I wanted Cody to hug me or maybe hold my hand.

But he didn't. With a quick wave, he jogged across the sand toward his house. He passed the ATV parked in the driveway and disappeared around the back of the house.

I shimmied up the square corner column from the lower porch to the upper one, threw my leg over the back porch railing, and landed on the porch floor. Trying to be as quiet as possible, I tiptoed past the sliding door to Stephanie's room, peeked in, and saw her dark hair tumbled on the pillow. Still asleep.

She'd never have to know.

An inch at a time, I opened the sliding door to my room and slipped in. In only a few seconds I had changed to Dad's old Heineken T-shirt that I always wore to sleep in and slid under the covers, pulling them to my chin. Fine, grainy sand coated my feet and legs next to the sheets. For a time I lay there catching my breath and staring out through the sliding door at the dawn sky.

It looked like we'd gotten away with it.

But every time I closed my eyes, I saw the mare, the one they'd called Isabel, lying on the beach, panting. I saw Dark Angel, the scared little black foal. I thought I'd never sleep again.

14

STEPHANIE

Again, strong morning sun shone through the sliding door, heating my room and waking me up. I had slept later than usual, and my arm had an awful, sore, stinging feeling. It hurt even more when I sat up and tried to pull my T-shirt on. Brownish blood had seeped through the bandage, making it stick to my arm. I tried pulling the bandage off, but it hurt so bad my eyes watered. So I just left it.

I went out on the back porch to look at the ocean,

and below I saw a red fox trot by on dainty feet, its bushy tail hanging low. Before I could call Diana to come see, it skulked through the grasses on the dune, until it wove through a few stalks and disappeared like fog.

I usually slept later than Diana, so I was surprised when I peeked into her room and saw her still sleeping. One sandy foot stuck out from under the covers along the side of the bed. Then the thought popped into my head like a newspaper headline: *Diana snuck out last night.*

I could hear Daddy and Lynn downstairs talking, and I stood and listened for a minute at the top of the stairs before going down.

"He's a very handsome boy, and he seems bright," Lynn said. "It's no wonder Stephanie is fascinated by him. He's different from most of the boys she knows."

"Stephanie is too young to have anything to do with boys," Daddy said with sudden force.

"Oh, I agree. But you can't stop her from being interested," Lynn said. "Once it happens, it just happens."

"I can keep her away from them."

"No, you can't, Norm! There are boys in her school, on the teams she cheers for ... Boys are everywhere! Are you going to keep her prisoner in a castle turret like Rapunzel?"

"Yes!" said Daddy, laughing. "I think Rapunzel's dad had the right idea!"

"Right!" Lynn said, with a soft chuckle. "And I'm sure Rapunzel and her dad had a wonderful relationship."

"Who cares about our relationship as long as she's safe?" Daddy said.

"Oh, Norm, you don't mean that."

"No, you're right, I don't," he said.

"Besides, honey, as hard as you might try, you can't protect her from a broken heart," Lynn said. "She's already been through your divorce and our marriage, and that will make a girl wise beyond her years."

I waited a few heartbeats and then walked downstairs rubbing my eyes like I'd just gotten up. "Morning," I said.

"Morning, sweet pea!" Daddy said a bit too enthusiastically. He stood and gave me a hug. "Did you sleep well?"

"Mmm-hmmm."

"How's your arm?" Lynn asked.

"It stings, and the bandage is stuck."

"I can take care of that." Lynn sat me at the counter while she got the first-aid kit. With a quick practiced swipe, she yanked off the bandage.

"OW!" My eyes watered.

"It's easier if you do it quickly," she said, holding

my arm gently in her confident hands. She cleaned off the dried blood with warm, soapy water. "It looks better today."

The wound felt tender and raw, and tiny pinpricks of fresh, bright red blood appeared. I felt more secure as Lynn placed a new, smaller bandage over it. "By tomorrow, we should be able to leave it open to the air." She patted my arm. "I can't believe Diana is sleeping so late. That's unusual for her."

"I know," I said vaguely. "Weird."

"Somebody needs to wake her up. We've got a lot to do today," Daddy said. "I've been checking out the websites for both the aquarium and the Wright Brothers Memorial."

"Stephanie, do you mind running over to the Clarks' and seeing if leaving around ten will work for Cody?" asked Lynn. "That will give us time to get Diana up and get some breakfast."

"S-sure." I would have liked a chance to comb my hair before going over there, in case I saw Cody, but after overhearing Daddy's conversation with Lynn about me and boys, I thought it would be better if I acted like it didn't matter, so I skimmed down the front steps and headed across the packed sand to the yellow house. I passed the ATV in their driveway and quickly combed my hair with my fingers before knocking on the doorjamb.

I'd been hoping Cody would come to the door, but it was Mrs. Clark.

"Hi!" She smiled. Her brown eyes were warm and friendly. The aroma of pancakes wafted from inside the house. Mrs. Clark said she was making sea cookies, one of Cody's favorites. I asked her if ten o'clock was a good time for Cody to head over to go to the aquarium, and she said yes. I tried not to crane my neck to see if Cody was anywhere in the room behind her.

"I've got to get Cody up," she said with a conspiratorial smile. "He's usually an early riser, but for some reason this morning he's sleeping in."

That was funny. Cody and Diana *both* sleeping in this morning.

"Okay, see you in a bit!" I said, without commenting or letting my expression change, and turned to run back across to our house.

And just then, a police car pulled into the sand-packed driveway. An officer got out, slamming the door, and stepped up onto the front porch.

I stood rooted to the porch. *What's going on?*

"Can I help you, sir?" asked Mrs. Clark, wiping flour off her hands.

The officer stepped forward to shake Mrs. Clark's hand. "Morning, ma'am. Sergeant Lloyd Stone. How are you this morning?"

"Fine," said Mrs. Clark warily. "Is there a problem, sir?"

"A horse was hit on the beach late last night by somebody driving an ATV." The sergeant was stocky and muscular, with almost no hair, and carried a shiny black gun. "I'd like to take a look at this ATV." He stepped back into the yard and circled the ATV, with his arms crossed, looking real carefully at the tires and body. Then he snapped a few pictures of the ATV using a camera with a long lens.

"Well, that's impossible," said Mrs. Clark. "No one was driving this ATV last night. I'm quite sure."

"I'd like to ask you and your family members some questions, if you don't mind."

Mrs. Clark knitted her brow. "Well ... I would never let Cody drive the ATV at night. And everyone in our house was in bed by midnight last night."

"Someone called 911 from a cell phone in the wee hours of the morning to report an injured horse but hung up before identifying themselves." The sergeant gave a cell-phone number and said it was registered by Malia Clark. "Is that you?"

Mrs. Clark put her hand over her mouth. "That's Cody's phone. So, you're saying he was out on the beach last night and made a call to 911?"

What? Cody called 911 last night?

"I'm saying that phone was used to call 911. I'd like to speak with Cody, please."

Mrs. Clark glanced at me, and her face had turned pale. "Stephanie, maybe you should go home. Please tell your parents that the earliest Cody can make it today will be ten-thirty, and he may not be able to make it at all."

"Yes, ma'am." I started across the sand, warm now beneath my bare feet.

"Wait, we'd rather you didn't leave, young lady," said the sergeant. "Were you out on the beach with that young man last night?"

"No, sir," I said, in sudden shock. A roaring started in my head.

"You're sure about that? The voice on the recorded 911 call was female and sounded about your age." The sergeant loomed closer to me now, taking off his sunglasses and squinting at me thoughtfully in the bright sun.

"I'm sure," I said in what I know was a scared voice.

What happened last night? Did someone use Cody's phone to call? Was Cody out on the beach? Was he with Diana? Did they hit a horse with the ATV?

"Where are you staying, young lady?"

I pointed at our house. "Over there." The blood had gone to my head, and I kind of felt like I was going to faint.

"And how do you know this young man?" The sergeant leaned against the car, patiently, holding the camera.

"We met on the beach, that's all. We just started talking, and he offered me a ride on the ATV."

"You realize that in this county you have to be sixteen to ride an ATV? Are you sixteen?"

My mouth dropped open. "No, sir. I don't think Cody knew that either."

"What happened to your arm?"

I cupped my other hand over the bandage. "I scraped it when I fell off the ATV yesterday afternoon."

"Some people I've interviewed did say that they saw some young people driving an ATV behind the dunes in a somewhat reckless manner yesterday afternoon. Was that you and Cody?"

Someone told the police that they saw Cody and Diana and me on the path when we fell off the ATV?

"Well," Mrs. Clark glanced at me. "That was purely an accident, and this young lady can certainly assure you of that, can't you, Stephanie?"

I nodded. "Yes, ma'am. It was an accident. Cody was really sorry."

The sergeant regarded me with his narrow eyes. "All right. You go on home, but I'd like you and your family to stay put so we can ask you some questions in a few minutes."

I looked back at Mrs. Clark, and she gave me a nod.

"And now I'd like to speak with Cody," said Sergeant Stone to Mrs. Clark.

"Just a moment, I'll get him," she said. "I'm sure this is all a big misunderstanding, and we'll be able to straighten it out very easily. I know Cody didn't hit any horse." She turned to go back inside. I started running back to our house, my heart beating all out of time.

As I was running, my brain was whirling like crazy trying to figure everything out. Had Diana snuck out last night and somehow ended up hanging out with Cody? I just couldn't believe it, since Diana had said more than once that she didn't even like him. And she knew how I felt about him! So why would she do that?

And if they'd been riding the ATV on the beach last night, it seems like we would have heard them.

I turned around and looked at Cody's house just in time to see Mrs. Clark go inside with the sergeant. And he was going to be over here soon, as soon as he talked to Cody. And what would Cody say to him?

A hot breeze blew, whistling around me, stirring up the sand and whipping the sea grass. My hair stung as it blew into my eyes, and I raked it away.

I slowed to a walk as I got to the yard at our house. The more I thought about it, the madder I got at Diana. How could she have sneaked out with Cody? And when had they planned it?

She was so tough to get along with, and I had tried so hard. I'd gone along with what she wanted to do last summer and gotten into trouble with the wolves. I'd tried to be loving toward her, and now look!

I went inside and quietly closed the front door. Daddy and Lynn were in the great room, facing the ocean, and wouldn't have seen the sheriff's car unless they came to the front door and opened it.

"There you are!" Lynn immediately began cracking eggs into a bowl.

"Stephanie, what took you so long?" Daddy said, looking up from his computer.

Diana was sitting at the counter, eating cereal, in that old, faded Heineken T-shirt of her dad's.

"Sorry." I stared at Diana, willing her to meet my eyes, but she was either paying no attention or purposely avoiding looking at me. In that very second, I was almost sure: she had sneaked out with Cody, and she was trying to keep it a secret from me.

Well, I wasn't going to keep her secret.

"A policeman is over at the Clark's house," I said in a really calm voice. "A horse was hit on the beach late last night by an ATV, and he thinks Cody did it."

"What?" Lynn, who was stirring eggs, stopped. Daddy stared at me. Diana, though, just kept eating, which completely convinced me.

"And the person who called 911 from Cody's cell phone was a girl."

Now, like a shot, Diana looked up at me, holding her spoon in midair. Her mouth was open and her eyes burned into mine.

15

DIANA

Oh my gosh! How could Stephanie do that to me? Come in and announce that!

After our whole adventure with the wolves last summer, after all we'd been through. And she'd always been on my side!

Suddenly it hit me. She was mad about Cody. Thought I planned to sneak out with him from the beginning.

"A girl called? What girl? So what does that mean?" Mom said.

"It means that a girl was with Cody last night when the cell phone call was made about the horse," Stephanie said. "The policeman asked us to stay here because he wants to come ask us some questions," she added.

"Us? Why us?" Norm demanded. "We had nothing to do with that."

"Is the horse okay?" I asked. "Did the horse live?"

Everyone in the family stopped. Looked at me. Mom put both hands on the counter, a look of shock on her face. "Diana?"

"What?" Then I turned to Stephanie, glaring. "Thanks a lot! Thanks for being so loyal!" I threw my spoon into the bowl.

"What were you doing with Cody?" Stephanie said.

"It was just coincidence. We didn't plan it."

"I don't believe you."

"So the person who made the middle-of-the-night cell phone call to report the injured horse was *you*?" Mom screeched.

"I'm going upstairs." I couldn't believe Stephanie had done this to me. I jumped off my stool and stomped toward the staircase.

"Now you wait just a minute, young lady!" Mom said.

"You're not going anywhere," said Norm. "You're going to sit on this couch and explain this to us before the policeman gets here."

If I could have thrown a bucket of paint in Stephanie's face right then, I would have. To tell on me, just because of a boy. I was too mad to sit down; there was no way I was going to do what Norm told me to do. I just stood at the foot of the stairs. My head felt like it was going to blow off.

"We didn't do anything! We just found the horse. It was already injured. We weren't on the ATV, we were riding bikes."

"In the middle of the night?" Mom said.

"I wanted to check on that wild horse that was injured. It wasn't the middle of the night; it was just really early in the morning, about five or six."

"You know better than to go out at that time without telling us where you're going."

"What were you doing with that boy?" Norm asked.

"I just ran into him on the beach, and he wanted to come with me." I gave Stephanie a look of vindication. "I didn't even want him to come. I told you I didn't really like him." I wasn't going to admit to her that my feelings for him had changed, not now. I really wasn't sure how to deal with that myself.

"And he wanted to come anyway?" Mom asked.

I nodded. "Yeah."

Stephanie gave me a smoldering, skeptical look.

"I don't care if you don't believe me," I said to her.

"It's the truth. He rode your bike." I pulled at a string from the hem of dad's old T-shirt. "What did they say about the horse? Is it okay?"

"They didn't say," Stephanie said.

"Diana, are you telling us the truth?" Mom said.

"I'm not a liar!" I yelled. "I can't believe this. There was an injured horse! She needed us! Maybe we saved her life! And all you guys can do is yell at me!" That was it. I ran up the stairs to my room and slammed the door.

I started to lie down on my bed but went outside on the porch instead and stood looking out at the beach, smearing the tears off my cheeks with the heels of my palms. My brain buzzed with anger at everyone, and my heart pounded. I let the sun dazzle my eyes and listened to the surf and tried to do what my doc had said, which was to slow down my breathing and try to rate my mood. Moronic Mood-o-Meter nine point five, maybe even ten. Terrible.

I tried to see down where the mare and foal had been on the beach but couldn't see that far.

Mom would come upstairs to talk to me now, I knew she would. Maybe we shouldn't have been out on the beach at that time of night, but Cody and I didn't do anything wrong. What we did was good.

As usual, nobody ever saw the good in what I did.

I couldn't wait to be a grown-up and make my own decisions.

Well, maybe I just wouldn't wait around for the cop to come ask me a bunch of questions. Maybe I'd just climb over the porch railing and leave. That would show them. Maybe I'd just go stay at Dad's. He'd support me. He didn't have a bunch of ridiculous rules about everything.

I sat on the bed and put on a pair of shorts and a T-shirt. I was tying my running shoes when there was a knock on my door.

"Diana?" Mom came in. Her face looked very serious. "We need to talk about last night in detail before the police get here. I don't know what kind of crime it is to hit a horse."

"I told you, I didn't hit a horse! I didn't do anything! I called 911! That's all I did!"

"It's just that the policeman is going to be looking for the person who did it, and you're going to have to have a solid story proving you didn't so he'll believe you."

"What do you mean? I'll just tell the truth? Won't the truth be good enough?"

Mom blinked and looked at me levelly. "I hope so."

Only a few minutes later, the police car drove up and parked behind Norm's car, and Norm went to the door.

"Good morning, officer," Norm said, shaking his hand. "Please come on in and sit down." He waved his arm at the couch.

Stephanie and I sat on the stools at the counter. I could feel waves of hatred coming from her and avoided looking at her or talking to her. My brain was still buzzing with anger, but my mouth was dry too. Why did everyone always assume that I had done something wrong?

"Thank you. Sergeant Lloyd Stone," said the officer. I recognized him from last night. He made a lot of noise coming in, with his boots and keys. A black gun gleamed on his belt. He took off his sunglasses and put them in his shirt pocket, then got out a really small laptop.

"Can I offer you some coffee?" Mom stood by the counter and nervously wiped it with a sponge.

The sergeant shook his head. "Thank you kindly. I'm fine, ma'am. I'd like to ask some questions, if you don't mind." He looked at Stephanie, then at me, then at Stephanie, then back at me again. He had a squarish, lined face that seemed kind. "Last night a horse was hit on the beach. Those of us who live around here care pretty strongly about protecting them. Hitting one of these horses is considered a hit-and-run misdemeanor and is punishable by a hefty fine. We need someone to help us understand what happened."

"Is the horse okay?" I blurted out.

"It's touch and go right now, and we hope she will be all right," the sergeant said. "But it could have been an entirely different story."

My heart squeezed with horrible pain, and I put my hand over my mouth. A sob escaped, and my vision went blurry. "Thank goodness!" I breathed.

"Oh, that's a great relief," Mom said.

"What about the foal?" I choked out.

"The herd manager hopes to save the foal too." The sergeant looked at me thoughtfully. "I take it you were there last night?"

"I found her on the beach. She was trying to get up." I couldn't seem to stop crying. Every time I pictured the mare, struggling on the beach, I felt so bad for her, then I felt relieved. I couldn't stop crying.

"So, why don't you tell us what happened?"

I swallowed my tears and cleared my throat. "Well, I was with this guy, Cody, and when we found her, I borrowed his cell phone and called 911."

"I see. So you reported the injured horse. And then what did you do?"

"I hung up."

"Why did you hang up?"

I looked at the floor. "Because I had sneaked out, and I didn't want anyone to find out about it."

"I see." The sergeant pursed his lips together thoughtfully. "So, how did it end up that you and Cody were together last night?"

"I just ran into him on the beach, and he wanted to come with me."

"So he was already out on the beach when you got there?"

"Yes."

"He could have been out there for several hours before you got there."

I thought about it. "I don't know how long he'd been there. But when he wanted to come with me, I finally said okay, and then we got the bikes and rode them down the beach."

"Where were you going?"

"I'd seen another horse that had been bitten by a stallion earlier in the day, and I wanted to check on it."

"In the middle of the night?"

"Well, early in the morning."

"Did Cody tell you why he was out on the beach in the middle of the night?"

"He said he couldn't sleep. He was hoping to see some bioluminescence in the water."

"Bioluminescence," the sheriff repeated after me, raising his eyebrows. He looked at Stephanie. "Can you tell me about the accident?"

Stephanie's eyes went wide, and then she said again, as she'd said so many times before, "It was just an accident. He didn't mean for it to happen."

She went on to describe the accident. Now that I wasn't answering questions myself, I saw that the sergeant was typing notes on his laptop.

"How did you meet this boy?"

"Just talking on the beach, that's all," Stephanie said. "I thought he was nice," she added. She didn't look at me.

"We never would have let her ride his ATV if she'd asked permission," Norm added quickly.

The sergeant looked back over at me. "So, anyway, you ran into the boy on the beach. Did he have the ATV with him?"

"No."

"And you said you wanted to go check on that other horse, and he said he wanted to go with you? Did he say why?"

"No. He just wanted to go."

"And as soon as you found the horse, you called 911. And then you hung up. Then what happened?"

"We hid in the sea grass to make sure that someone

came to take care of her. We watched you and the guy from the horse fund and the vet come up, and we saw the vet shoot her with the tranquilizing dart. Then we left."

"Why did you hide?"

"I told you, because I had snuck out and didn't want my parents to know I was out there."

"So you weren't hiding out of guilt for what you knew the boy had done earlier on his ATV."

"No!" I said.

"How do you know he didn't hit the horse earlier, before you ran into him?"

I stopped to think. "He would have acted differently when we saw it. He was just as surprised as I was."

"But you don't know for sure that he didn't."

I pushed my lips together tightly and glanced at Stephanie, then at the sergeant again. Answering that question might make it seem like Cody did it. I didn't want to answer.

"Diana, you need to tell the sergeant the truth now," said Norm in a warning voice.

"I am!" I sent Norm a smoldering look and felt a flash of anger. He thought I was thinking about lying! "I just am almost positive he didn't hit the horse," I said.

"Okay. Thanks." The sergeant reached for his sunglasses as he got to his feet. "I may need to ask more questions later."

"Cody is a nice guy," Stephanie said impulsively, starting to follow the sergeant to the door. "He wouldn't have—"

"Stephanie, let the sergeant do his job," said Norm. "You really barely know that boy."

"Thank you kindly," said Sergeant Stone. "We have your contact information, and we'll be back in touch if we need to. Meanwhile, if the young ladies can remember anything else that might be relevant, let us know."

"We will," said Norm, holding the door for the officer.

We sat in silence when the engine roared to life and the cruiser backed out of the driveway.

Then, just as I expected, Mom gave me a lecture on sneaking out and told me I was going to be grounded from the barn for another week after we got back from vacation.

"I guess we're not going to the aquarium with Cody, then, are we?" Stephanie asked.

Norm and Mom looked at each other.

"If we don't go," Mom observed, speaking mostly to Norm, "they might think that we believe Cody is guilty."

"Well," said Norm, "we don't know whether he is or not."

"But this is America, and in America you're innocent

until proven guilty," Mom pointed out. "I think we should go ahead with our plans."

Norm looked at Mom thoughtfully, then nodded and stood up. "Okay."

"I'll go over and make sure he still wants to go," said Mom, looking at her watch. "Girls, go get yourselves ready." She went down the front steps, and I watched through the screened door as she headed across the sand to the yellow house.

Without saying a word to Norm or Stephanie, I went up to my room and shut the door. I lay down on the bed and pictured the mare lying helpless on the beach last night. Again I could hear her moans, and I could see Dark Angel crying. Thank goodness they were okay so far.

I didn't want to go to the aquarium or the Wright Brothers Memorial. All I wanted was to help the horses.

Stephanie's footsteps sounded on the stairs, and her bedroom door opened and closed. I heard her closet door open, and the sliding sound of her dresser drawer.

I couldn't hold back. I darted across the hall and pushed open her door. "Thanks a lot for getting me in trouble!"

Stephanie's mouth flew open. "Well, you got Cody in trouble—by dragging him down the beach with you and using his cell phone to call 911."

"I didn't drag him! He wanted to come!"

"Girls!" Norm said in the sternest voice I'd ever heard him use. He came to the foot of the stairs. "That needs to stop right now."

I went back in my room and slammed the door.

16

STEPHANIE

We had to drive back over the bridge onto Roanoke Island to get to the aquarium. The whole way over, Diana and I sat in complete silence, as far away from each other as we could. Cody sat in the middle, between us. The only conversation was when Diana begged to find out how the mare and foal were doing. Daddy was silent, with his hands tight on the steering wheel, and I knew he was really mad.

Finally Lynn called the Wild Horse Fund herself and

said, "Hi, I heard about the injured mare and her foal and was just calling to find out how they're doing." She listened for a minute and then repeated, "Both all right so far. Touch and go. Thank you." She gave Diana a look and shut her phone.

Diana just burst out crying and turned her head to the window.

When we got to the aquarium, I got out of the car and waited, squinting in the sun, for Daddy. Diana got out and stood with Lynn, who put her arm around her and gave her a tissue. I'd wanted to do this, but now it was going to be awful. Cody looked totally depressed. He wouldn't look at me, and to tell the truth I didn't want to look at him either. Why had he sneaked out with Diana? Had they planned it before? It was hard to believe they'd just run into each other.

My feelings were so hurt. The two of them out last night running around the beach together, and me alone in my room not knowing anything about it.

Cody kept his hands in the pockets of his hiking shorts and just looked at the ground.

Daddy paid for our tickets and then said for us kids to go ahead through the aquarium, and that he and Lynn were going to catch up with us. We wandered away, but when I turned around and looked back, I saw Daddy and Lynn talking, and I knew they were discussing last night and the visit from the police.

I watched Cody and Diana. Did they seem different together? Did they exchange looks? Where they friends now ... or something more?

Stop it! I told myself. *Stop thinking like that.*

In the entrance to the aquarium was the jawbone, full of teeth, of a sixty-foot great white shark. It was huge, the size of an easy chair. We stood around awkwardly, reading the information about it. Diana walked away without saying anything to either Cody or me.

In the first room were coastal freshwater tanks, with a gross-looking giant salamander with an eel-like body, as well as a giant catfish with whiskers. Two small tanks held snakes that Cody was checking out. A cottonmouth, the sign said, the only venomous North Carolina snake that can swim, and a whitish colored rattlesnake with black diamonds. Both snakes were stone still, looking at us with unblinking eyes. I watched, waiting for one to move, but neither one did. It was eerie. Maybe the snakes could feel the tension between the three of us.

The next room had wetlands and a high glass roof like a terrarium. Diana was already in there, watching the otters swim back and forth, weaving their slim, brown bodies through the water, leaping out, racing through their den, then diving under the water again. When Cody and I approached her, Diana left the otter exhibit and moved to the alligators, obviously trying to get away from us.

After that was a separate room for sharks, and in the next room was a round central tank where stingrays swam with their flat sides up against the glass, flapping their wings. And guess who walked in? The two boys we'd seen riding ATVs yesterday! I could feel my face start to get hot the minute I saw them.

The boys didn't see us at first. I overheard Buzz Cut say to Curly, "I'm afraid of my dad. Are you?"

"Kinda," Curly said.

Then Buzz Cut and Curly started playing with their cell phones, laughing at something.

"Hey," I said to Diana and Cody. "Check it out."

"Uh-oh," Cody said. "Those guys."

At that instant they both looked up, saw us, and started laughing.

We walked away quickly and focused on a small tank nearby that contained a yellow octopus with eight delicate arms. An aquarium volunteer, a heavy-set bald man with glasses, sat next to the octopus as the three of us stood in front of the tank and looked. A Mr. Potato Head lay at the bottom of the tank next to the octopus.

"We put Mr. Potato Head in there with all his attachments—arms and legs and eyes—and she took him apart. She's very intelligent, and she loves to play. She's like a puppy dog," said the man.

"Really?" Cody said, interested. It was true—Mr. Potato Head was missing everything. His eyes and legs were scattered around among the stones on the bottom of the tank.

"She is so much fun to watch," the man said.

"That's amazing. I didn't know octopuses were playful," I said. I thought it was sweet the way the man had become attached to the octopus.

"She's a year old, and they only live for two years. I imagine she won't be with us much longer," the man added wistfully.

A sign on the tank said Do Not Tap on the Glass. Someone behind us reached out, with a snicker, and tapped the glass. I turned around and saw it was Curly.

The volunteer said, "No, no! That sign is serious. That octopus is very easily stressed. If she gets stressed, she turns red, and sometimes she'll release blackish-blue ink."

Diana darted over toward the boys. "Been riding ATVs much at night lately?" she hissed at them.

"What are you talking about?" Buzz Cut said. He gave her an angry look.

I could feel my heart beating wildly. Diana thought the boys had been the ones to hit the horse. Could they have done it? We *did* see them chasing the horses on the ATVs. I was embarrassed, so I walked away and stood in front of a small tank, trying not to listen.

"What's your problem?" Curly said to Diana. Then he went back to the octopus tank. "Hey, let's see if we can get this octopus to squirt black ink."

"That's enough, young man," said the volunteer. "I'll not have you harassing the octopus. Move along, please."

"Hey, Diana," I said, heading for the next room. "Come on!" I hoped to distract her from the boys. She glanced at me and didn't speak, then gave the boys a dirty look and walked with me to the next room.

The next room held a huge tank called the Graveyard of the Atlantic. About five sharks glided through the water, around and around a sunken submarine replica. I wondered how many times the sharks did that every day. The big tank made a humming sound that made me feel jumpy. Smaller fish shaped like torpedoes slid by the glass. Their round eyes, angled in their sockets, staring at us. A dark gray fish with a large head and whiskers swam by.

The three of us stood in front of the huge tank, looking in. I held myself very stiff, and the tension between us felt like a force field. The two boys appeared in the doorway of the room, but when they saw us, they ducked out.

"I'm so glad that horse is all right," Cody finally said to Diana.

And I knew what had brought them together. It was what they had shared last night with the horses.

Waiting to see if Diana answered, I caught her furious face reflected in the glass of the aquarium. Then she saw me looking and walked away, leaving Cody and me alone.

Cody sighed. "Did the cop ask Diana a lot of questions?"

"Yes," I said. I looked at him, trying to control the emotion on my face. "Did they ask you a lot too?"

"Yes." He nodded. "They think I hit the horse. It was so hard listening to that horse in pain in the dark. The sheriff asked me over and over again why I was out there. He didn't believe I was looking for bioluminescence." He looked down the hall in the direction Diana had gone.

"She's mad at me," I said.

"Why?"

"Because I told on her," I said. Now I was ashamed I'd done it.

"Why did you tell?"

Because I had a crush on you and was jealous. Of course I couldn't tell him that. I just shrugged and stared at the shark tank. A yellowish green eel with an evil smile slithered out of one of the submarine's algae-caked portholes.

"They would have found out anyway," he said. "I told them I was there with her."

I nodded, feeling a little better. "Diana thinks those guys did it."

Cody looked at me but didn't say anything. Then, when he spoke, he changed the subject. "You're stepsisters, right?"

"Yeah."

Cody nodded. "I have two stepsisters at my dad's house. They fight all the time. About everything." He grinned and spread his arms wide to show the wide array of topics his sisters fought about.

I laughed. "That sounds like me and Diana!"

He waved his arms. "I stay away! Danger, danger!"

I laughed again.

"But seriously, most of the time they're fun."

And just like that, the tension between us was broken. His gaze, when I looked at him, was completely open.

"Should we look for Diana?" he asked.

And it occurred to me that maybe he didn't "like" either Diana or me. Maybe we just reminded him of his stepsisters.

"Sure." I turned away and headed back toward the

entrance of the aquarium. I didn't know what had happened to the two boys, but it was a relief, because I didn't see them again. Finally we spotted Diana outside, standing at the edge of the sound. A low gray cloud smudged the horizon, and a chill wind blew off the opaque gunmetal water. Diana's shoulders were hunched over, and her skinny arms were crossed over her chest.

Should we go after her? She was always starting some drama and expecting people to come running after her. What if we just didn't? What if we left her out there wandering around? That would serve her right.

But, without even discussing it, Cody and I headed out toward Diana and the shoreline. The water was choppy, and we could see, in a haze, an arching bridge in the distance.

I was thinking about apologizing to Diana when my cell phone rang. I thought it might be Daddy, wondering where we were, but it was Mama, just calling to see how I was doing. I stopped to talk to her, and Cody walked on.

"Are you and Diana gettin' along okay?" she asked. I could picture her in the kitchen, or out in a lawn chair by the pool.

"Fine," I lied. Last time I told her about fighting with Diana, she called up Daddy and yelled at him. I wasn't about to tell her anything like that again—not about falling off the ATV, about the horse getting hit on the beach—nothing.

She started telling me about going boating with Barry and then to a college graduation party for one of his friend's sons—and as I listened I watched Cody catch up with Diana. He tried to talk to her, but she walked away. Was Diana mad at him too? I'd thought she was only mad at me.

"Honey, do you think you can stay with Daddy and Lynn for a few extra days after you get back from the beach?" Mama was saying. "Barry has a layover in New Orleans, and I want to go down and spend a couple of days with him."

"Sure, I'll ask." In fact, I was going to ask to stay with them permanently. Or at least I had been planning to until all this happened with Diana. Would Diana not want me to live with them now?

Cody was following Diana now, and finally she turned and listened to him, and started talking to him, and then I could tell that she was crying. They must have been talking about the horse.

I told Mama I had to go, then hung up. I stood at the wooden railing and watched Diana and Cody. Next to the water, the grasses moved, making a clicking, rushing sound in the invisible breeze. I had so many confused feelings about everything—about where I was going to live, about how I was going to get along with Diana, about the police coming today to interview us. I took a deep breath. Then another, and another, until I felt myself relax slightly. After one last deep breath, I followed the walkway to where Cody and Diana were. Heading that way, it became suddenly clear to me: the thing that Diana was really mad about was the horse getting hurt, not me telling.

And the second thing that came to me was this: we had to get Cody out of trouble, and the only way to do that was to find out who really did hit the horse. And to do that, we had to work together. Maybe it was those other two boys. Maybe we had to come up with some way to prove that they did it.

As I came up, Diana stopped talking, tossed her head, and started to walk away, but I grabbed her arm. "Diana, stop! Look, I'm sorry I told on you. It was wrong of me. But we need to stop fighting."

She knitted her brows and shot a look at Cody. "It's obvious *why* you told on me."

"Why?" Cody said, glancing from one of us to another.

I really hoped she wouldn't tell him why. "Well, I said I was sorry," I said quickly. *Please don't tell that,* I thought. "Now the main thing is to find out who *did* hit the horse. And how can we do that? There's got to be a way," I said. "And we can't keep fighting with each other. We have to work together."

Nobody spoke for a minute. We just stood together, as the wind whistled through the grass and a seagull flew by, calling plaintively. A short distance away, a long-necked great blue heron lifted into the air, flapping its big, triangular wings as if in slow motion, its spindly legs pointing straight out in back the way a superhero flies.

Diana studied my face, with her eyes narrowed, then took a breath and put her hands on her hips. "I bet it was those two guys we just saw in the aquarium." She looked at Cody. "Did the policeman say he was coming back?"

"He said he might have more questions. He took pictures of the ATV to see if it showed any damage."

"So the ATV that did it might have damage?" I asked.

"Yeah, I guess so," Cody said.

Diana said, "So when we get back this afternoon, we need to look for the ATV that did it. One of those guys had an ATV the same make and color as yours," she said to Cody.

"We should ride our bikes around the neighborhoods until we find it. If it takes us the rest of the week," I added.

The tension was broken at last. We stopped and got sandwiches and salads, and then went to the Wright Brothers Museum. Lynn and Daddy seemed to have talked about everything in the aquarium, and by now they were calmer and were joking around with us. They were holding hands, and I thought that was a good sign.

The plane inside the visitor center was a copy of the Wright Brothers' plane, since the original is in the Smithsonian Institution. It had broad glider wings made of white cloth stretched over a frame of amazingly thin strips of wood. A model of a person who was supposed to be Orville Wright was lying on his stomach near the small engine. We went outside and walked over to look at the house and hanger that the Wright Brothers used. The hanger wasn't really any bigger than a garage. Their house had a ladder inside that they climbed to get to the sleeping loft, and an old-fashioned stove inside for heat. I bet they were freezing, because their flight was in December and I was cold today and this was April. The distances that the brothers had flown on their first four flights in 1903 were marked out on the sandy ground behind the visitors center.

We went outside to walk the distances, but it was so windy and flat, and I felt so relieved not to be fighting with Diana anymore that I just ran to the first marker, with my hair whipping in the wind and my jacket making a flapping sound. Then Diana ran to the second marker, which was a tiny bit farther, and Cody ran to the third, which was a little farther than that. We all ran together to the fourth marker, which was much, much farther, almost a thousand feet, or a fifth of a mile. After that we ran across the field and up a hill, on curving paths, to a huge white stone memorial. Up there, in all directions, we could see Nags Head and Kill Devil Hills. The wind was crazy, blowing our hair straight up in the air, pasting our jackets against us or billowing them out. We could see the ocean on one side and the sound on the other.

"There's a reason why the Wright Brothers chose to come here from Ohio," Daddy shouted when he and Lynn joined us. "All this wind!"

Diana and Cody decided to race down the hill from the memorial back to the visitors center, which must have been a mile. I offered to be the starter.

"On your mark, get set, go!" I dropped my arm and they took off, their skinny legs flashing like scissors. Diana was matching Cody stride for stride as they ran down the hill. She was running the fastest I've ever seen her run, straining to beat him, but as they passed the halfway mark, Cody started to pull ahead. I ran along behind, to try to stay close enough to see who won, and I started yelling at the top of my lungs into the wind.

"Go Diana! Go! Come on, you can do it!"

She put on the steam, lengthened her stride, and almost caught him, but then at the end he leaned forward and kicked in a burst of speed and ended up beating her by about five yards.

I couldn't even run the whole way, it was so far, and when I got there, they'd both collapsed and had laid right down on the ground, out of breath and laughing. So I fell down onto the warm, sandy grass too. It felt so good not to be fighting anymore, and to have a plan to help Cody.

17

DIANA

Funny how mad I had been at Stephanie before, and now I wasn't. She'd told on me, but so had Cody. He'd had to tell the truth to the police sergeant. And what Stephanie had said, about helping Cody by finding out who really hit the horse, had made sense. Really doing something to help the horse was so much better than running around just being mad. It was funny that Mom and Norm were suddenly okay with us hanging out with Cody, mostly to prove to Cody and his mom that we didn't think he was guilty of hitting the horse.

And since last night my feelings about Cody had completely changed.

Back at our house, Stephanie texted Cody and said to meet us out by the turtle's nest. We were rushing out onto the beach with our bikes to meet him when Mom stopped me, her cell phone in her hand.

"I thought I'd call your dad, Diana, and double-check to make sure everything is on for tomorrow. Why don't you wait a minute before you go bike riding?"

"Do I have to?" As much as I wanted to see Dad, I didn't want to listen to Mom talk to him. If he wasn't going to be there tomorrow, I didn't want to know right now. Besides, we only had a couple of hours of daylight to search for the ATV.

Mom cocked her head and looked at me with suspicion. "You're not even interested in talking to your dad on the phone?"

"I just talked to him yesterday. I'll see him tomorrow." I headed down the walkway, a hand on each handlebar, as Mom yelled for us to be back by dinnertime at seven–thirty. Stephanie was right behind me. We stood near the turtle's nest with our bikes, waiting for Cody. The tide was low and the sun was just above the trees in back of Cody's house, throwing long shadows on the beach that made us look like girls on stilts and our bikes look like the ones in the circus with gigantic wheels. A cool late afternoon breeze ruffled the hairs on my arms. With sharp cries, a few seagulls landed near us and strutted across the sand, waiting to see if we had any food.

"I can't believe you didn't want to talk to your dad," Stephanie said.

"We have a lot of searching to do before dark." It had also occurred to me that going to see Dad would mean Stephanie and Cody would be together without me for a whole day.

"I get it," Stephanie said. She was redoing her shiny, dark ponytail, something she did almost every hour.

We didn't have to wait long before we heard the rumble of the ATV engine. Cody flew over the dune, airborne, and then landed and skidded to a sideways stop. The seagulls scattered.

"*Hola,*" he said.

"Whoa!" I laughed, and Stephanie kind of jumped back with a little squeal.

"Okay," he said. "What should we do? Should we split up or what?"

"I don't like to be by myself," Stephanie said.

"Let's stay together. We can go up each path from the beach together and investigate the houses in each neighborhood."

"And what are we looking for?" Stephanie asked.

"An ATV that's damaged. And it might be hidden somewhere, like inside a garage, especially if the guy thinks the cops are looking for him," I said. "If we find one, we'll take a picture of it with a cell phone to show to the police."

"Okay!" Cody said and gunned the ATV motor.

Stephanie and I jumped on our bikes, and the three of us headed down the beach. At the first path through the dunes, we rode as far as we could on our bikes, and when the sand became too soft to ride through, we dropped them and continued on foot. Cody continued on the ATV, driving slowly so he wouldn't leave us behind.

Three houses were arranged around a sand cul-de-sac. Like our rental houses, the driveways were no more than packed-down sand. No ATVs were in sight, and none of the houses had garages. We headed back to our bikes, rode down the beach to the next neighborhood, and repeated the pattern.

"This is going to take a long time," Stephanie said, wiping sweat from her temple as we rode up the path to the third set of houses.

Later we passed the place on the beach where it had all happened. High tide had washed away most of the hoof prints and tire tracks, but above the waterline we could still see some. We stopped and stood there in the darkening light for a few minutes, without talking. I thought about the thing that had happened there. I could hear the mare's groans again and see her trying to lift her head, with Dark Angel neighing and pacing nearby. The sounds of their pain were so vivid in my memory.

Cody took off his helmet and held it in his lap, bowing his head.

"Come on," I finally said. "Let's catch whoever did this."

We scoured five more neighborhoods but found no ATVs. A couple of houses had large storage areas underneath them, where an ATV could be hidden, but we didn't go up to the houses because some people were still coming in from the beach, carrying beach chairs, umbrellas, and bags with bright towels. We didn't want to be arrested for trespassing.

The sky turned indigo, and a cool breeze threaded through the sea grass. I was covered with sand and sweat, and the muscles in my legs ached. We hadn't glimpsed a single ATV, and we hadn't seen any of the wild horses either. Since the accident they seemed to have melted into the woods and disappeared.

"It's getting dark, and I'm tired," Stephanie complained as we picked up our bikes from the foot of a dune about a half mile past where the accident had occurred. We'd searched all the houses along the beach for at least a mile and a half, and it was becoming clear to us just how many houses and how much distance would need to be covered. And acres and acres of dunes and woods stretched further inland, all without roads.

"This is impossible," Cody said, cutting the engine on the ATV. He gestured to encompass our surroundings. "We could search all week. A whole year."

"We can't give up!" I said, practically crying. How could we? Yet I was feeling completely discouraged and overwhelmed by the size of the project we'd taken on.

"We have to go back," Stephanie said. "Daddy and Lynn are going to be really mad at us if we're late. We're in enough trouble already."

"We can start again tomorrow," said Cody.

I didn't want to tell him that maybe I wouldn't be there tomorrow. I thought about Cody and Stephanie spending the whole day together without me. I almost hoped Dad forgot.

"I wish we knew where those two guys lived," I said. I was beginning to realize that it was one thing to suspect someone had done something and another thing to be able to prove it.

Stephanie and I turned our bikes around and began

riding back down the beach, with Cody slowly riding alongside on the ATV. The tide was low, and parts of the beach shone with translucent, rainbow-colored puddles where the surf had been moments before. Lights popped on in the houses as dusk deepened and shadows stretched over the sand.

We hadn't been riding long when we saw two horses running down the beach near the water. One was light-colored and the other was chestnut. As they ran by, their long tails rippled in the evening breeze.

"Hey, look!" I said, turning to watch them. "That's Firecracker! He's found a friend! He's not alone anymore! He's found a new herd! That's fantastic!"

The three of us watched for a few moments as the two horses cavorted on the beach in the dusk. They seemed to be dancing, ducking their heads and coming together, and then galloping along neck and neck. Then a third horse raced up to join them.

Other people walking on the beach stopped to watch and admire the horses.

"Yay!" Stephanie said. She stopped and turned a cartwheel on the sand. What a show off. But I wished I could do one. Then I thought, *Why not?*

"Hey," I said. "Show me how to do one!"

"Okay." She showed me how to hold my arms up high and to follow my arms around with the cartwheel, pointing my toes and letting them wheel around with gravity.

"You're coordinated and athletic. That's good!" she said after my first try. I practiced doing two or three more, each a little better than the last.

"Great!"

As a joke, Cody tried one too. It was awkward.

"You look like a frog," Stephanie said, laughing. "Standing on its head."

Cody did another one with his legs even more bent.

"A sick upside-down frog," I said.

"Thank you very much," Cody said, using an Elvis accent.

The light was fading now, and we turned on the flashlights we'd brought. The air was cooler, and I zipped up my sweatshirt. The sand felt cool under my feet. Crabs skittered across the sand in front of our flashlight beams. The stars were starting to come out, and the sky was splashed with their brilliance. On the moving surface of the water, there seemed to be a sparkling path to the moon.

"This would be the perfect time for bioluminescence," Cody said. "I wish there was some tonight."

"There is," I said, pointing to a lightning bug that floated past us, slowly flashing on and off.

"Are lightning bugs considered bioluminescence?" Stephanie said.

"Well, actually, yeah!" Cody said.

"Why do they light up?" Stephanie asked.

"I don't think scientists know for sure. Some say it's to attract a mate."

"And how do they light up? And don't tell us we wouldn't understand this time," I said in a teasing voice.

"It's caused when lightning bugs release a little bit of luciferase, and it reacts with ATP and luciferin. They have a special organ where the chemical reaction takes place. When one of the chemicals runs out, their light turns off."

"When I was little and Mom and Dad took me to church sometimes," Stephanie said. "We sang this song in Sunday school called 'This Little Light of Mine.' That's what the lightning bugs make me think of. The idea that there's a light inside each one of us."

"Cool," I said. "Mom takes yoga, and after a yoga class they say '*Namaste*,' which means 'the light in me honors the light in you.' Kind of the same idea."

"*Namaste*," Stephanie said to me. Then she turned to Cody and said it to him.

"Ditto," Cody said.

The triangular window in front of our house was lit.

"We'll meet you out here tomorrow!" Stephanie said to Cody. He waved good-bye and drove behind the dune to the path to his house, and we walked our bikes up the walkway, their wheels making a rattling sound on the wood.

We opened the sliding doors, and Norm was sitting on the couch in the great room, watching the news. "There you are!" he said.

We smelled fish cooking and saw Mom in the kitchen. She turned around.

"Did Dad cancel?" If he did, I was ready to find out now.

"Nope. We're meeting him tomorrow at ten by Jockey's Ridge. He's got big plans, apparently," Mom said, but she raked her hair off her face in a way that I knew meant she was nervous. So was I.

18

STEPHANIE

A full-length mirror hung on the back of my bedroom door, and before climbing into bed, I studied my reflection. Suddenly the door pushed open, smashing me against the wall. Diana came in, wearing her father's Heineken T-shirt and carrying a deck of cards.

"What are you doing?" she said, throwing herself on my bed.

"Do you think I've lost weight this week? Maybe because we've been riding bikes so much?"

"I don't know," Diana said. She sounded bored. She shuffled the deck of cards in a smooth, practiced way, making them whir like a little fan. "Who cares? You look at yourself in the mirror way too much."

"I do?"

"Yeah! It's annoying. I mean, everyone already thinks you're gorgeous. You don't need to play it up. It makes you seem stuck-up or something." She started laying out the cards to play Solitaire on my blue bedspread.

"I'm not stuck-up!" I said. I liked looking in the mirror because I hadn't been "pretty" until just a year or so ago. Suddenly boys liked looking at me, and I felt like I had to check to see why. And to tell the truth, sometimes I looked in the mirror to figure out who I was. Sometimes, especially lately, with Daddy and Lynn getting married, and trying to get along with Diana, and Mama marrying Barry, and the stuff at school, my mind went through so many changes that I felt like I had to look at myself to make sure I was still the same person. Almost as though I had to check to make sure I hadn't disappeared. But that was too much to tell Diana. I put my pink nightgown on and started brushing my hair, suddenly thinking that Diana probably thought I brushed my hair too much too. Well, I thought, looking at her scraggly, matted, blonde ponytail, Diana brushed hers too *little*.

Outside the open sliding door, through the screen, the surf made sounds that were almost quiet and reassuring, like someone saying, "Shhh. Shhh."

"So, since you and Cody were together last night, you haven't seemed so negative about him," I said. I poked Diana in the leg with my hairbrush.

Maybe she'd tell me what had gone on between them.

"He's not so bad," she said abruptly.

"Is that all you can say? He's not so bad?'"

"Yes."

"And what did he do to make you change how you feel about him?" I asked.

Cards snapped as she built up piles of each suit at the top of the columns, ending with a king at the top of each pile.

"I won!" She pushed the piles together and began shuffling again. "I don't know. We were together when we found the horse. " I'd seen her crying when she was talking to him at the aquarium, and I'd seen him put his hand on her arm.

I tried not to be jealous. But I still was, a little. But then, when we were at the aquarium, I understood that Diana and I just reminded Cody of his stepsisters, and maybe he didn't like either of us.

I decided to change the subject.

"So, what do you think you and your dad are going to do tomorrow?"

She finally stopped shuffling and put the cards on the nightstand, then crawled under the covers, pulling them to her chin. She talked not to me but to the ceiling.

"I'm going to guess that we'll do something dangerous that he thinks I'll love but my mom won't let me do." She turned on her side, facing me, and propped her cheek on her elbow, speaking earnestly. "I don't want to talk about him anymore. Listen, what kind of person do you think hit the mare? Who would do that?"

At that moment Daddy knocked on the door and poked his head in. "Just thought you girls might want to know that Lynn just called the Wild Horse Fund again, and there's no change in the mare's condition. She is hanging in there, but she's not out of the woods." He drummed his fingers on the doorjamb, then left.

"God can't let Isabel die! I don't know what I'll do!" Diana said.

"Oh, so you believe in God now," I said.

"I guess I've been thinking about God more since last summer with the wolves," Diana said. "But mostly I've always thought that we're on our own in this world. No one really cares about anything but themselves. You live and then you die. That's it." She hesitated. "What about you? Do you believe in God?"

"Yeah, I guess I do. Maybe God isn't in charge of all the good and bad things that happen in the world. You have to admit, it was a person who hit Isabel, not God."

"But who would do that? Hit a horse on the beach and leave it lying there?"

"I have no idea, Diana." I let my eyes wander around the room as I thought about the possibilities for a minute. "Maybe the person who did it was drunk or on drugs and just really messed up." I picked at a string on the comforter. "I mean, I know some people do evil things on purpose. But I bet it was an accident.

"That's what I think too. And do you think this person feels guilty? "

"I don't know. I mean, I hope so. *I* would."

"Let's say he feels terrible about what he did, and he doesn't want anyone to find out that he hurt the horse. Let's also say the ATV is damaged from hitting the horse—so what would he do? Would he ride the ATV in public?"

"No. He'd hide it," I said.

"That's what I think too. So it's hidden somewhere. So where's the best place for a person to hide an ATV around here?" Diana's thin, serious, freckled face was only inches from mine on the pillow. Her water-washed blue eyes, as she looked at me, were intensely focused. "Where do you think that is?"

"Uh … out in the wilderness, where the horses are?"

"Bingo. And that's where we've got to look. We probably were wasting our time looking around the houses today. So tomorrow you and Cody need to go out in the dunes and the woods behind the houses and look for another ATV."

She kept on talking. I watched her lips move and nodded my head. I was scared of the woods behind the houses. I was scared of riding the ATV again. I knew two people weren't supposed to ride at once. I was scared of the wild horses, and I didn't want to do any of it. But I kept nodding my head until she went back to her own room.

After that there were cracks of thunder and streaks of lightning. I listened to the shrill of the wind through the trees. Rain pattered on the roof and sifted through the tree leaves. I drew in the fresh smell of the rain coming through the open windows.

At some point I fell asleep.

19

DIANA

Mom and I sat in the parking lot by Jockey's Ridge, waiting. The lot was beginning to fill up, and people were piling out of the cars, slamming doors, laughing, yelling, and filing down the sandy path toward the dunes, which rose behind us like sleeping giants. The sky was an impossibly bright, clean color of blue today after last night's storm. I thought about the fact that because of the storm, all of the evidence of the accident with Isabel was now washed away.

Mom looked pale, and she kept picking at the cuticles on her fingernails until she finally made her thumb bleed. "Shoot," she said, putting her finger in her mouth. She took it out and examined it.

"He could have gotten stuck in traffic." My mouth was dry and my lips felt chapped. I could barely form the words.

I had the deck of cards, and I'd brought a pillowcase with Dad's old Heineken T-shirt, a change of clothes, a bathing suit, a towel, and a toothbrush just in case I ended up spending the night. But I felt all mixed up. If Cody and Stephanie found the damaged ATV, they probably wouldn't know what to do without me. They needed me there with them. I really wanted to see Dad, but I really wanted to be there with Cody and Stephanie. If only I could clone myself or be two places at once.

I needed a cell phone in case I had to call them and tell them what to do.

As if Mom read my mind, she handed me her cell phone. "Here. Take this today. And here's Norm's cell number." She scribbled Norm's number on a page of her Day-Timer, and when she handed it to me, a bit of blood from her torn cuticle smeared onto the paper.

"Mom, I know Norm's cell. And it's stored in your phone anyway. He's, like, number one on your call list."

Mom blinked. "I know, I know. I'm just a little nervous, that's all."

As soon as Mom left, I'd text Stephanie to see what she and Cody were planning to do to find the ATV.

Mom pulled a twenty-dollar bill out of her wallet. "And here. Take this. You never know when you might need it."

"Thanks." I folded the bill and put it in the back pocket of my shorts.

Mom drummed her fingers on the steering wheel. "Hmmm. What else? Obviously if he tries to take you skydiving or something like that, you just say you can't." She gave a high-pitched, fake-sounding laugh.

"I think you have to be eighteen to skydive. Anyway, I'm going to be fine," I said roughly.

"I know, I know. I hope you and your dad have a great visit." She reached to brush my hair back from my forehead. I looked away, so that she was brushing air. "I'll be here promptly at five o'clock to pick you up. Make sure you call me if you're going to be late for any reason. And, just call me halfway through the day to let me know how things are going. Just so I won't worry."

"Mom, you'll worry no matter what. So what difference does it make if I call you?"

"Diana, call me. I mean it."

At that moment a silver convertible car spun into the parking lot and came to a screeching halt at an angle next to us. I glanced over, cringing slightly.

It was Dad, just hanging up his cell. He jumped out of the car and opened our passenger door. "Dudette! How great is this, that we get to spend the day together?"

I have never been a touchy-feely person. I slid out of the seat and kind of stood there while he hugged me and gave me several hearty, nervous pats on the back. Mom always described him as the kind of guy who could sell ice to Eskimos. His nickname in high school and college was "Motor," short for "Motormouth."

"We had a breakfast session that went long this morning, people just listening to themselves talk ad infinitum." He was tall and skinny and energetic, with reddish gray hair and piercing green eyes. He and I have the same eyes and freckled skin. He had a loud voice, and when he walked he had loud footsteps.

Mom had jumped out of her side of the car and come around. "Hello, Steven," she said.

"Lynn. You look absolutely fabulous," he said, his smile widening.

"Oh, thanks." Mom cleared her throat, looked down, and jangled her car keys. "So"—she gestured to the convertible—"this a rental?"

"That's right! I figure when I'm renting I might as

well rent something decent that I actually want to drive. It'll be fun for Diana. We can spend the morning together. Then I have to go back to the resort for some ad-hoc meetings, so I figured Diana could keep herself busy at the pool. Do you have your bathing suit?" He patted me on the shoulder. I guess he meant for it to be a pat, but it was more like he was hitting me, the way referees hit the wrestling mat during a match.

"Yeah." I held up the pillowcase.

"So, there will be time when you can't be with Diana?"

"It won't be long, just a quick meet and greet," Dad said. "She's fourteen. She'll be all right."

"Sure," I said.

Mom squinted at him. "So, what are you going to do?"

"Well, I've been thinking we'd go for the veritable all-sports day," Dad said, squeezing my shoulder. "Start out with a little hang gliding here at Jockey's Ridge? And maybe move on to some jet skiing or parasailing later? What do you say, dudette?"

"Sounds cool to me!" I smiled in spite of the lameness of the *dudette*. Jet skiing last summer had been a blast. And I'd never gone hang gliding, but it looked fantastic. All the stuff Dad had mentioned was expensive. It made me feel like Dad was willing to spend a lot on me.

"Hang gliding?" Mom said uncertainly.

"It's perfectly safe," Dad said. "They teach kids as young as four years old here. I checked it out."

"Let's go, Dad!" I said. Time to separate them. I grabbed my pillowcase and jogged with it around Dad's car to the shotgun seat, which was full of a briefcase, printouts, brochures, and a box of business cards.

"Just throw your stuff on top. We'll move it later," Dad said. "Wait, hand me one of those business cards."

I opened one of the boxes and pulled out a card, then handed it to Dad, who ceremoniously presented it to Mom. "How about we meet at the resort where the conference is? You know where?"

"Yes. Five o'clock, then," Mom said in a firmer voice than usual. "At the resort. And we all have each other's cell numbers. Diana, be sure and give your dad Norm's number."

"I will, Mom." Her nervousness was making me nervous. I couldn't wait for her to leave. She came over and looked like she was going to hug and kiss me, but I gave her a warning look, so she just kissed her index finger and put it on my forehead, smiling at me with searching eyes.

And within moments, Dad and I were alone.

"Okay," he said. "We sign up for hang gliding lessons down this path here." He squeezed my shoulder again. "So, tell me what's going on in your life, dudette."

He'd never asked me that before. I took a deep breath, felt a little tingle run down my spine, and began telling him about life at the barn, Josie the barn manager, and the personalities of the different horses there. Started to tell him what it was like to live with Norm, and part-time with Stephanie.

Dad's phone buzzed. "Hang on," he said, then answered. "Yeah? No, I should get commission on those. Absolutely." He held up a finger to me to say "wait one minute," and then stopped on the path. "I did all the legwork on those cases. Those sales should be mine."

We stood aside for two people to pass us. Dad finished his conversation, then turned back to me. "What were you saying?"

I picked back up where I left off, and as we followed a winding path to the visitors center, I told him about Stephanie coming to my school, and how popular she'd become. I told him how lame it was that we had to memorize poems over spring break. I was about to tell him about some of the kids calling me "animal" in the hall, but then we arrived at the visitors center. Two people stood in line ahead of us to sign up for hang gliding lessons.

For hang gliding you have to go to "ground school" first. I went in a movie room with a bunch of other people—kids and adults—and we watched a video where a guy talked to us about how to control the glider.

"The dunes are a great place to learn because if you wipe out you land in the soft sand. It's almost impossible to get hurt," the instructor said.

Dad didn't go with me to ground school, and when it was over, I couldn't find him. Finally I found him standing outside the visitors center talking on the phone. I told him we were supposed to hike out to the dunes and meet my instructor, who was taking the glider up the hill. There would be four other people in my class, and we would each get five turns at hang gliding.

"So, are you excited? This is the chance of a lifetime," Dad said as we headed across the sand. "Yeah!" As we climbed the first dune, the wind picked up, whistling in my ears, plastering my T-shirt against me, and whipping my ponytail around. The view from the top of the ridge, from one side, looked like we were walking through a desert. Then, when we crested the ridge, on the other side were acres of dunes, Highway 158, rows of houses, and beyond those, the deep blue of the ocean. Both adults and kids ran along, harnessed under the blue and white glider wings, with an instructor running alongside, holding on to a rope attached to the glider, to launch them. Someone had brought along their golden retriever, which excitedly galloped along, racing the gliders as they skimmed the landscape. A couple of kids were rolling all the way down the side of the biggest dune. It looked like a blast. As Dad and I climbed the ridge, I watched one guy about my age take off and get a long ride—probably eight to ten whole seconds—from the top of the dune all the way to the bottom. Then I watched another boy tip forward and wipe out in the sand within ten feet of taking off.

I wasn't going to wipe out. I would show Dad what a good athlete I was.

Someone had written "SOS" in huge letters in the sand on the side of one dune that could be read from the sky.

That was when I remembered that the whole morning had gone by and I hadn't gotten in touch with Stephanie. I quickly texted her and told her that I had Mom's phone and to text or call me and let me know how things were going.

"You go, girl!" Dad said, giving me another hard pat on the shoulder as the other students and I gathered around the instructor.

My instructor was a guy named Al, about sixteen or seventeen, with curly brown hair to his shoulders. He'd been hang gliding for six years. We hiked across the sand behind him to a flat spot for our first ride. I was a little confused how we were going to hang glide on a flat area.

My group, which consisted of three other kids my age, and a grown-up couple, all put on harnesses and helmets, the way Al showed us. My first ride was not what I expected. It wasn't really even a ride; we just had to balance the glider as we ran along a flat area of sand. But balancing the glider wasn't as easy as it looked. The glider wasn't that heavy, but you couldn't let it tip either forward or backward. Tipping it back before you were ready would make you start to take off, and tipping it forward tended to "stall" it, or make it dive into the ground.

Then Al showed us how to foot launch along that same flat area, by running along with the glider balanced but angled slightly up to catch the wind and then picking up our feet and letting the glider carry us. For hang gliding, you have to pay attention to which way the wind is blowing so that you launch with the wind, not against it. I got only about a foot off the ground for the first ride, and only flew about twenty feet or so.

To turn the glider right, you have to move your hands to the right side of the glider bar and push your hips and legs to the right so you're actually shifting your weight. To turn the glider left, move your hands over to the left side of the glider bar and shift the weight of your hips and legs to the left. When you land, you're supposed to be flying into the wind and uphill, so that you're slowing down.

Finally, on our fifth flight, we had to practice taking off with the wind and flying downhill for about eighty yards. Al carried the glider back uphill for all of us.

I got in line last because I wanted to watch the others and learn from their mistakes. The boy who went before me smoothly executed the entire ride, landing on his feet at the bottom of the hill. He dropped the glider and held his arms up in victory, and we all cheered for him.

Then it was my turn. I planned to do exactly what that boy had done. I really wanted Dad to be impressed.

I lifted the glider by the front bar and made sure it was centrally balanced over my shoulders. I didn't look back at Dad. I ran along carrying the glider with my hands evenly spaced on the bar, and then ran the first few feet down the dune and launched myself, pulling my feet up under me and tipping the glider slightly backward to catch the wind. It caught! I sailed about ten feet off the ground toward the bottom of the dune.

What a fantastic feeling! I was flying! The wind whistled by, and the ground gradually dropped farther and farther away. But for some reason—maybe because I'm left-handed—the glider started diving toward the left.

Suddenly I heard Al beside me yelling, "Straighten up!"

I tried to react quickly, but I overreacted, and the glider lost momentum and stalled, hooking left and diving into the sand three-quarters of the way down the hill. I landed on my feet but then fell down, crashing the glider into the sand. I wasn't hurt—just mortified that Dad had seen me wipe out.

Al took the glider from me, telling me not to be embarrassed, stuff like this happened all the time. He dragged the glider back up the hill, and I trudged back up behind him, with sweat rolling into my eyes and sand filling my running shoes.

When I got to the top of the hill, the two boys my age were laughing at me, and Dad was nowhere in sight.

Al called me a trouper and then said that our lesson was over, encouraging us to rent a hang glider sometime soon and practice the skills we'd learned. I trudged past a couple of other groups getting lessons and finally found Dad on the phone again. He was arguing with someone. "So did you talk to them? Somebody needs to talk to them."

I waited for a while, until he hung up.

"So? How'd it go?" he said.

I realized that he hadn't been watching me at all. "Great!" I lied.

"Come on," Dad said. "We're out of here."

We trudged down the hill and through the valley.

"Sorry," Dad said. "Business is tough these days. I'm in a very competitive line of work."

It was a long walk back to the parking lot, like hiking across the desert. Wind swirled sand so it stung my calves, and the sun glared in my eyes.

My stomach growled, and I felt light-headed. I had been too excited to eat early this morning before we left, and the lesson had been over three hours long. Occasional black spots drifted in front of my eyes. I hadn't noticed until now, but I'd scraped my shin when I wiped out, and blood was running down my leg. I licked my finger and wiped off the blood.

Two seagulls flew overhead with shrill cries, and down by the visitors center, a little kid was screaming because he didn't weigh enough to take a full hang gliding lesson and had to go in the kids' group. A hot wind kept blowing.

"Come on," Dad said again. He put his hand on my back and pushed me forward, to speed me up, and I kind of stumbled.

"Okay," I said. I felt like crying. I hadn't felt this way in such a long time, and I'd thought those memories were gone. But it was amazing how quickly those same old feelings came flooding back. I checked Mom's cell phone to see what time it was. Almost one o'clock. Four more hours with Dad.

I got a text from Stephanie and opened it.

> Daddy and Lynn made me spend the morning memorizing my Elizabeth Barrett Browning poem. Cody and I are getting together later.

So wherever the ATV was hidden, no one was looking for it. And whoever had hit the mare was still getting away with it.

Disgusted, I shoved the phone back into my pocket.

Dad got into the car and started it. He waited impatiently while I moved the business cards and other stuff to the backseat so I could sit shotgun. He stared ahead with his hands gripping the wheel.

"So ..." he said. "I've had enough of this place. Now what?"

"I'm kind of hungry."

He cocked his head, nodded, and backed out of the parking space at warp speed, then headed north. As he drove, he seemed to become lost in thought. I figured he was thinking about a place to stop to eat.

"This conference I'm attending is giving us all kinds of new marketing techniques for selling insurance online. It used to be we sold insurance based on relationships. Now it's all based on search engines. It's frustrating for the kind of person I am, a people person. I say put me in a room with a human being, and I can make a sale. But this online stuff is a whole different animal."

"Right," I said.

We drove almost all the way back to where our house was, and then we pulled into a resort with hotel rooms and condos on one side of the road and a pool and spa on the other. I could hear the laughs and screams of kids in the pool as we turned in.

"Here we are!" Dad got out of the car, slamming the door. "I'm going to drop you off here at the pool—I'll sign you in—and run over and make an appearance at the meet and greet. I won't be gone too long. Looks like there are a lot of kids there. You should have fun."

I got out, wondering if there was any food here. I fingered the twenty-dollar bill in my back pocket. I could at least buy a sandwich if I needed to.

Dad went up to the lifeguard at the counter by the front gate and showed his room card. The gate opened, and I went in.

"See you in a bit!" he said, and then jogged across the parking lot and went inside the lobby.

On the way to the women's room, I saw a hot tub labeled Teen Hot Tub, and about five kids around my age sat in it, laughing and joking. The girls wore expensive bathing suits and had pedicures. Stephanie would probably have just walk over and said "Hi." I, on the other hand, ignored them.

I found the women's room and changed into my bathing suit. I didn't like going shopping, so this was a Speedo that Mom had bought for me on sale at the end of last summer. A bin with a stack of huge fluffy white towels stood beside the door. I took one and went out to the pool. I picked a chair that was off by itself. The sun was glaring hot, and the chlorinated water in the pool flashed white in my eyes. I got out Mom's phone and tried to think of someone I could text.

Stephanie was the only person I could think of. As much as she drove me crazy, and as much as I had been mean to her, she was the one. So I wrote her, asking if she and Cody were looking for the damaged ATV yet.

She answered right away. She said she was still stuck reciting her poem with Daddy and Lynn. And I realized that she had truly become someone I could count on. Right then I wished more than anything that I could talk to her.

I closed the phone and stared at the bright water in the pool. Black spots started floating across my vision. I wondered again if I could get some food here. The twenty-dollar bill Mom had given me was still in my shorts pocket.

I looked around and saw the counter where food was served. Two high school girls, dressed in white, were waiting on people. I went over. I pulled the twenty out of my pocket and said "Excuse me" to the girl standing closest to me. She had smooth brown hair and almond shaped eyes with a thin line of blue eyeliner around them, making her eyes look huge.

"How much is a Coke and a cheeseburger?"

"We don't take money here," she said. "You have to charge it to the room."

"I have twenty dollars. Can't I just pay for it with that?"

"No. We don't have any way of taking money."

"Oh." I tried giving her Dad's name, but she insisted that the room number was what she needed.

"Thanks."

I went back over to the side of the pool. I sat down and let my feet swing over the water, rubbed the blood off my leg again, then felt kind of faint and shaky and lay down. The sun shone through my closed eyelids. Here, I was just waiting, and I had no power over anything.

I must have fallen asleep for a few minutes. I heard the faint sloshing of the water against the tiles on the side of the pool and opened my eyes. How much time had gone by? I jumped up.

Black spots bloomed in front of my eyes, and the sky whirled. My arms helicoptered, and I fell over the edge into the shallow water, landing on my back with a soaking splash. "Whoa!" I yelled, swallowing water, scrambling to my feet. The water was only about two feet deep.

All the kids in the hot tub started laughing.

What an idiot.

I thought about it. We had passed a restaurant a ways back on the road. I could walk back there.

I didn't bother to try to find Dad. Why should I? What did he care? I just headed across the parking lot, listening to the squish of my shoes and the gravel crunching under my feet, squeezing the water out of my ponytail.

"Diana!" Dad came out into the parking lot yelling.

I kept walking. What did I owe him?

"Hey! Where are you going?" He stopped and gestured as if he couldn't believe what he was seeing.

I wheeled and yelled back at him. "What do you care?"

I continued my march toward the highway and looked up and down the road. A lot of the businesses around here weren't open yet for the season, and I saw a lot of empty parking lots. But a block away, on the other side of the highway, was a gas station. I could get a Coke and some kind of sandwich there. Maybe they had fries. I was dying for some fries. It would be hard to find a break in the traffic, though. Cars flew by at a blur.

"Diana!" Dad came up behind me, grabbed me by the elbow, and swung me around.

"Let go of me!"

"I will not! What are you doing?"

"I'm hungry, all right? I need something to eat!"

He tightened his grip on my elbow and pulled me away from the street. "What's the matter with you? Why didn't you tell me you were hungry?"

"I did!" I wasn't going to cry. In fact, I was too mad to cry. "But you didn't listen!"

20

STEPHANIE

"**O**ne more time, sweetie, and then you can head out to the beach," Daddy said. We were on the back porch. He and Lynn sat close together on a chaise lounge, holding hands, and he wore his sunglasses, squinting at my printout of the Elizabeth Barrett Browning poem "How Do I Love Thee?" as it flapped and crackled in the sea breeze. It was supposed to be one of the most famous love sonnets ever written. Elizabeth Barrett Browning wrote it for her husband, Robert Browning, who was also a famous poet.

"But I only made two little mistakes!" I said, shaking my foot to jiggle one flip-flop, in a hurry to get to the beach. We'd promised Diana that we'd look for the ATV! She'd already texted me, asking if Cody and I had found anything. "Besides, Diana hasn't practiced hers at all yet."

"You be concerned about your own work, not hers," Daddy said.

"I love the fact that you're memorizing a famous love poem," Lynn said. "I think I'll try to memorize it too, so I can recite it to your daddy." She leaned over and kissed Daddy on the end of his nose. Daddy turned and smiled at her, and even in the sun I could see him blush.

"PDA!" I covered my eyes and made a gagging motion, but secretly I liked seeing them joke around this way.

"Sorry, sweetie, we're listening," Daddy said, laughing, and he squeezed Lynn closer. I closed my eyes for a minute, pretending it was Daddy and Mama, but I opened them again quickly, knowing it was babyish to think that.

"Okay," I sighed. I cleared my throat and started out the poem again.

> How do I love thee? Let me count the ways.
> I love thee to the depth and breadth and height

My soul can reach, when feeling out of sight
For the ends of being and ideal grace.
I love thee to the level of every day's
Most quiet need, by sun and candle-light.
I love thee freely, as men strive for right.
I love thee purely, as they turn from praise.
I love thee with the passion put to use
In my old griefs, and with my childhood's faith.
I love thee with a love I seemed to lose
With my lost saints. I love thee with the breath,
Smiles, tears, of all my life; and, if God choose,
I shall but love thee better after death."

"Perfect!" Daddy said. "Good job, sweetie."

I had wanted to memorize this poem because my teacher had told me about the famous love story between Elizabeth Barrett Browning and Robert Browning. Elizabeth was born in England in the 1800s. She wrote her first poem when she was twelve. At that same time, she was learning Greek, Latin, and Hebrew. She was passionately religious and wrote about things like slavery, the rights of women, and child labor.

When she was fifteen, she was bedridden with some mysterious lung or spinal disease that doctors never diagnosed, and they gave her morphine for the pain. She became addicted to the morphine, which I guess used to happen to people a lot back then.

She was already a famous poet when Robert Browning wrote her to say he admired her work. They wrote letters to each other for a long time, and he told her in a letter, before he even met her, that he loved her poems and he loved her too. When he finally went to her home for a visit, they fell in love in person. She could not believe that a handsome man like Robert Browning could love an invalid like her. Elizabeth's father wouldn't give his permission for them to marry, so they eloped. Her father immediately disowned her, and she never saw him again. For the rest of her life, she wrote her father letter after letter begging for forgiveness, but he never even opened them. I thought that was terrible. Her health became worse, and after fifteen years together with Robert, she died in his arms. After her death, Robert and her son published many of her poems.

Anyway, it was such a beautiful and romantic story. Would I find love like this someday?

Lynn had been reading over the poem, and she said, "Let me try now." She took a breath. "How do I love thee? Let me count the ways. I love thee to the depth and the breadth and height my soul can reach, when feeling out of sight for the ends of being and ideal grace." She stopped, then waved her hands with impatience. "I'm distracted." She picked up her phone and looked at it.

"I keep thinking about whether Diana might be trying to get in touch with me. I just hope things are going all right with her dad. Anyway, I wish I had a young mind! Look how easily you did that, Stephanie! I can't remember the next line."

"I love thee to the level of every day's most quiet need, by sun and candle-light."

I knew that line because I remembered it meant that Elizabeth loved him both by day and by night. I finished the poem again, feeling even prouder of myself.

"That's just great, sweetie."

"What do you think it means by the line 'I love thee with a love I seemed to lose with my lost saints'?" Lynn asked.

I had thought about that. "I was thinking that maybe she had faith in God when she was little, but then maybe something bad happened to make her lose her faith. I read online that her brother drowned, and she became very depressed afterward because she had a fight with him the last time she saw him, and they never really got a chance to make up. I think bad things happening can make a person stop believing in God." I thought about my conversation with Diana.

"Does the poem make it sound as though her love for Robert replaced her love for God?" Daddy asked.

I looked at the words of the poem again. "I don't

think so, because at the end she said that if God chooses, she'll love him even better after death. So she believed in God's will, and also in eternal life."

"So maybe her love for Robert revived her ability to love both God and others again?" Lynn asked.

"That's what I think," I said.

Lynn and Daddy exchanged a glance. "I could understand how that can happen," Lynn said.

A voice inside me said, *Ask them now. Ask if you can live with them.*

I opened my mouth, but then was too afraid. "How did y'all know you were in love?" I asked instead.

They looked at each other again and laughed, and each put a hand on the other's knee. "For me it was love at first sight," Daddy said.

"Oh, it was not!" Lynn said.

"Seriously, remember when I brought you flowers on our second date—"

"Daffodils and tulips!"

"—and the flower vase dropped on the floor, and I was trying to help you clean it up, and I cut my hand? The touch of your hands when you cleaned and bandaged mine … I'll always remember that. It made me fall in love. The touch of your hands."

Lynn put her hand on Daddy's cheek and kissed him on the lips.

"Okay, I'm going to the beach!" I said, grabbing the poem away from Daddy.

"Go ahead." Daddy and Lynn were both laughing.

I got my beach bag and headed down the wooden walkway to the beach, wondering what it would be like to fall in love. I mean, I knew I was really too young to be in love, but still, it was interesting to think about. I was only one year younger than Juliet was when she met Romeo.

I went to check out the little turtle nest and examined the soft, undisturbed sand in the little triangle outlined by the tape. Dozens of delicate, round eggs were hidden just a few inches below. It was way too early for them to come out. They wouldn't hatch until July, and it was only April. I headed closer to the water and stretched out on my towel, facing the waves.

I opened my phone. Two more texts from Diana! I texted her and said I was out on the beach, about to get in touch with Cody. I asked her how things were going with her dad. Diana didn't answer. Then I texted Cody telling him that I was on the beach. He answered that he would be here in a few minutes.

I started thinking, what did I know about Cody?

He seemed like he was from a middle class family like us. His parents were teachers and researchers. And he seemed really smart, as if his school might be harder than ours. I could tell his schoolwork was important to him, and that he studied harder than I did. I knew he was a caring person from the way he had acted about the injured horse, and I liked that. And he knew so much about biology and nature.

I checked my phone again. Still no text from Diana about her dad. She'd been so excited about seeing him after such a long time. Would he let her down again?

A shadow fell over my feet. I looked up. Cody. Wearing an OBX T-shirt.

"Hey!" I said, sitting up. "I was just texting Diana. She's texted me about three times, wanting to know if we found anything."

Cody laughed. "Well, we better get going so we can report back to Diana! Should we take bikes? I know your parents won't go for the ATV again."

"Sure." We headed back to the house. Daddy and Lynn, carrying their towels and beach bags, were getting ready to come down to the beach, and I told them we were going for a bike ride.

"You kids sure are riding bikes a lot this week," Daddy commented. "More than usual. Great that you're getting so much exercise on vacation."

"I have a hard time just sitting on the beach," Cody said, hopping from one foot to the other, as if to prove it. "I like to be doing something."

I just stood there and smiled vaguely.

As we were walking our bikes down the wooden walkway to the beach, our eyes met, and we were laughing. Then Cody looked down at the handlebars and pushed his glasses up on his nose.

Down on the beach, as we pedaled along, the waves roared beside us, and the sandpipers were funny, running like crazy away from our tires. Above us, in perfect formation, four pelicans glided by. The sun dazzled my eyes with its brightness, and I felt completely breathless.

Why did time have to go by? When you wanted to stop it, it seemed to spin by even faster, going by in an instant. Our vacation was almost over.

We rode in the water a little bit, sending a rainbow spray soaring. We hollered, "Woo-hoo!" And the wind caught our words and blew them away.

A few minutes later, we were riding down the sandy paths through the neighborhoods, stopping often to walk the bikes through deep, fluffy sand. We entered the maritime forest, staying on the path, with gnarled trees with twisting branches arching over us on either side. We had to duck to avoid tree branches and brace to bump over hills. The ground became dark and rich looking under the sand. Finding some paths that looked like they might be used for four-wheeling, we sped down them.

And then, as we emerged from a stand of trees to a small, sunny opening in the forest, we saw a harem of the wild horses, their heads down, grazing, with two little foals cavorting. When we rode up, the foals raced back close to their mothers, and the others turned their heads to look at us. They were beautiful! Within a few heartbeats, they whirled and galloped away from us, manes and tails flying. I wished Diana could have been here to see this with us.

"Amazing," Cody said, turning toward me.

"I hate that we scared them."

We followed the path to the end of the open space, walked our bikes a short distance, and found ourselves at the edge of a precipice, staring at a view that I had never dreamed existed here. Probably fifty feet below us, stretching to the horizon, lay a patchwork of marshland and maritime forests in a dozen lush hues of green. Gigantic live oaks stood like floating islands amid the carpet of green, and a wide stream wound its way through the center, the water so still it perfectly reflected the blue sky, white clouds, and green and gold grasses. "Wow," I breathed, taking it all in.

"Amazing," Cody said again.

"Look at the birds!" I pointed to a line of white birds, sparkling in the sun, rising from the marsh and into the sky, their cries drifting faintly up to us.

A few seconds ticked by, and then the scene was suddenly shattered by the earsplitting grind of ATV engines behind us, and Buzz Cut and Curly crested the hill. We caught snatches of their laughter as they flashed by. Because we had walked off the path and were hidden by foliage, they didn't see us.

"Hey, want to follow them?" I said to Cody.

"We probably can't keep up." Cody seemed nonchalant, as if he really was more interested in the view than our search.

"But Diana thinks they're the ones who hit the horse."

"They didn't hit the horse," Cody said. He cast his eyes downward, focusing on the ground.

"Who did it, then?" I asked. "We haven't seen anyone else around here riding ATVs."

Cody didn't say anything. Blood started to rush into my head with a roaring sound as I watched his face twist with guilt. He took off his glasses and cleaned them on his T-shirt.

"I did it."

I gasped and put my hand over my mouth. "What?" I could hardly get the word out.

He turned away from me so I was looking at his back while he was talking. "I wanted to see the bioluminescence in the ocean. I wanted to see what it was like to drive the ATV at night. I was driving and looking in the other direction, at the water, and just came up on her really suddenly, and clipped her back leg. She didn't even stop running, and I didn't know that she'd fallen until Diana and I went back. It didn't even damage the ATV … I hardly hit her at all."

I could barely concentrate on what he was saying. My thoughts began racing. "So you lied to the police, and to us? And you've been letting us spend half our vacation riding around looking for a damaged ATV? Why would you do that? Why wouldn't you just admit that you did it?"

No wonder he had said over and over how relieved he was that the mare was doing all right.

He sat down, cross-legged, and plucked a few strands of grass and began tearing them up. "At home, I'm the 'good' brother. My older brother has gotten into so much trouble. He's been suspended from school a couple of times. My mom sent him to stay with my dad because she couldn't deal with him anymore."

Just like Matt's mother sending him to stay with Barry and Mama. And me.

"I'm always feeling this pressure to be a decent kid. I have to get good grades. I have to be a good kid. Like my mom just can't stand it if I screw up."

"I get that," I said. I felt the same pressure all the time. "Still, you've been lying to us for days!"

"I know … I'm sorry. It was just an accident, a terrible accident, and I wouldn't have even known that anything bad happened if Diana and I hadn't gone back and seen her. "

I felt heavy disappointment, like I was about to explode. I had thought I liked him, that I knew him, and now this! I thought of Diana. She was going to freak! Absolutely freak! She'd never forgive him.

"I'm really sorry," he said again. "I'm going to have to tell my mom. It's such a relief that the horse is still doing okay."

I remembered the wolves.

"Last summer, Diana and I lied to our parents about releasing the wolves for two days, because we were afraid of what would happen when they found out. So I guess Diana and I have done almost exactly this same thing."

We sat in silence for a few minutes.

"You're going to have to call the cops," I said.

"I know."

Still, we sat and didn't move. Thoughts tumbled around in my mind. I relived our time at the aquarium, when Diana was blaming the other two boys. I relived our walk on the beach, when we were talking about the bioluminescence, the special light inside each one of us. It made me mad that he let us talk like that, knowing what he'd done.

Yet, we'd done exactly the same thing.

"Are you going to call the cops now?" I said.

He shrugged and cleaned his glasses again, though they hadn't had time to get dirty. Slowly he pulled his phone from his pocket. Diana had saved the number for the sheriff's office on his phone, and he punched it in. "I'd like to report accidentally injuring a horse on the beach," he said.

He ended up talking to Sergeant Stone, who agreed to meet him at his beach house in twenty minutes. So we pushed our bikes back out onto the path and rode toward home. The beauty of the spot we'd found had been lost and forgotten. We passed a small grassy area where the black earth had been churned into ruts and chunks, and I figured that those boys had done it on their ATVs. We kept on going.

When we got back to our houses, Sergeant Stone's car was already in the driveway. The car door creaked as he stepped out.

As Cody and I parked the bikes under our house, I noticed Daddy's car was gone. I watched Cody walk toward Sergeant Stone, with my heart beating so hard I had a pain in my chest.

"Good luck," I said.

21

DIANA

I sat across from Dad at one of the tables beside the pool. The kids in the hot tub had left. We weren't talking. I dipped french fries into the little cup of ketchup and shoveled them into my mouth like I hadn't eaten in weeks.

He had ordered a double bacon cheeseburger and was taking huge bites of it. "I just wish you'd told me you were hungry," he said without looking at me, in between bites. "I absolutely would have gotten you something to eat."

I got a lump in my throat the size of a golf ball, but I wasn't about to cry. I wouldn't let him see me cry. "We're eating now," I said.

The sun went behind a cloud, and it suddenly seemed dark.

"I know I'm out of practice with this kind of stuff," he said.

I twirled a french fry in the ketchup and looked up at his face. He had lines around his eyes, and his lips looked dry and cracked. He rubbed his big hand over his reddish-gray stubble in a tired way.

"My job is very demanding right now," he said. "I know it's tough everywhere. But I should have been more aware. I'm sorry."

When I looked at his face, he looked truly sorry. The thought occurred to me that he was probably trying to do his best.

Suddenly words spilled out of me. "I wanted to show you stuff, Dad. My whole life." I spoke calmly and in a normal voice. "You have no idea of what my life is like now. Today all I wanted was to show you how good I was at hang gliding, and you weren't even watching!"

He blinked, then wadded up the empty yellow wrapper from his burger. He looked across the pool, then back at me. Then his salesman personality came roaring back. "Hey, don't call your mom just yet, dudette."

"No, I think I want to call Mom." I got out the phone. I was tired of things always being the same with him. Maybe it wasn't too late to be with Stephanie and Cody.

"Listen, Diana, give me a second chance," he said. "Let's do something else together. " He picked up his drink cup. "I know. Let's go parasailing."

"Parasailing? You're kidding, right?"

"Not kidding."

And thirty minutes later, I was standing on the back of a boat, rocking on the sound with Dad and a couple of other people, wearing a heavy life vest and a harness and holding on to a handle behind a bar. Dad wasn't going to go, because it was expensive, but he wanted me to.

"We have a problem," said the boat captain. "With the low wind out there today, you're too small to go single. We need you to go tandem. Is there anyone here who will go with her?"

Some of the other people looked at each other, but no one volunteered.

"I will," Dad said without a moment's hesitation.

So he stepped into a life vest and harness and stood beside me, and we gripped the handles attached to the parachute behind the boat. I held my breath, and my chest felt tight. The captain hit the tiller, and we sailed up into the air so quickly and smoothly I almost didn't notice it had happened. We soared up and up, and the bay and the houses and the whitecaps shrank smaller and smaller until they looked like one of those scale models you sometimes see in museums, showing Civil War battles or historical views of cities. The air got colder and I felt breathless.

As we rose higher, the bay, which had been choppy with whitecaps, now looked perfectly smooth. We could see the hills of sand at Jockey's Ridge, and the green trees of Roanoke Island, and the tall white Wright Brothers Memorial, and on the other side of the long, thin banks, the ocean, stretching on forever.

"Look," Dad said. "You can see the curvature of the earth."

Down below, the boat with the others waving looked like a bathtub toy. I had thought that parasailing would be loud and scary, but it was quiet, peaceful, almost surreal. I looked over at Dad, and his expression was kind as he surveyed the dazzling landscape before us and then placed his hand over mine.

22

STEPHANIE

Last summer I had followed Diana, and she had been the one to do everything. Now I'd done something on my own. I'd persuaded Cody to call the police and confess what he'd done.

I still didn't feel all that great. I punched in the front-door entry code and went inside by myself.

"Daddy? Lynn?"

No one answered. On the counter, they'd left me a note. They'd gotten so worried about Diana spending the day with her dad that they had both gone to pick her up. They said they'd be back in time for dinner, and they wanted me to set the table.

I folded the napkins and walked around the table, placing the forks, knives and spoons at their correct places. Then I put the plates around. I was thinking about what Diana would say about Cody. She'd feel so betrayed. It was already so hard for her to trust people. Diana would think that I had betrayed her too.

For some reason I started thinking about people calling Diana *Annn-i-MAL*. I remembered a conversation I'd had with Colleen when she had visited Daddy's house that weekend. I'd invited Diana to play cards, and she'd said no in a completely rude voice. I'd been mad, and when Diana left the room, I said, "She likes animals more than people."

Could that be how the whole Annn-i-MAL thing started? Could that possibly be the reason? And with a sickening jolt, I knew it was true. Colleen must have told someone what I said, and then somehow it got twisted. Guilt flooded my entire body! The name calling had been started by something *I* said.

The front door opened, and Daddy, Lynn, and Diana came in carrying pizza boxes. Diana was sunburned, and her hair was tangled from the wind. But her eyes sparkled. Her visit had been good.

"Things went well with your dad?" I said to Diana. I dished out cups of water for everyone, my hands shaking.

"Yeah, it was really fun," she said.

I glanced at Daddy and Lynn, and they both smiled, a little bit cautiously.

"The day was a success," Lynn said, putting the pizza boxes on the counter. The smell was incredible. My mouth watered.

"That's great," I said.

"Thanks for setting the table, Stephanie," Lynn said.

"Let's eat!" said Daddy.

So we all sat down. Lynn had ordered one pizza with sausage and mushrooms, and the other plain, with extra cheese, the way Diana and I liked it.

"I went hang gliding and parasailing," Diana said. "It was amazing!"

Amazing. I thought of Cody. I was waiting for someone to ask about the police car next door, and I didn't have to wait much longer.

"Why is the police car over at Cody's house again?" Daddy asked.

I took a deep breath. "Uh … maybe Cody should tell you himself."

"What?" Lynn asked. "Why don't you just tell us now?"

I glanced at Diana, and our eyes locked. "Cody was

the one who hit Isabel," I said. "He was scared to admit to it because he didn't want to get in trouble. He told me while we were riding bikes today, and I made him call the police to report it. They were here when we got back."

Diana's mouth dropped open. Tears filled her eyes. "All that time," she whispered. "He lied to us all that time!"

"We did the same thing ourselves last summer, Diana, with the wolves," I reminded her.

"It's not the same! Isabel almost died! It's not the same! And he was lying to us!" Diana dropped her pizza onto her plate and got up from the table.

"Diana, I know this is upsetting, but there is no need to leave the table," Daddy said. "Let's finish our meal."

"How could I eat now?"

"You need to eat, honey," Lynn said. "We all do."

Tears ran down Diana's cheeks. "I knew I didn't like him! I knew it! I was right the whole time!" She ran upstairs and slammed her bedroom door, leaving the three of us to finish eating in silence.

After dinner, Daddy, Lynn and I were sitting on the couch, each of us reading, though I'd read the same paragraph four times, when Diana came downstairs. Her eyes were red, but she wasn't crying anymore.

"Sorry," she said, barely louder than a whisper.

Lynn got up and gave her a hug.

I wanted to hug her too, but I couldn't bring myself to approach her. *Annn-i-MAL* rang in my ears.

Daddy and Lynn suggested we recite our poems for them. I reluctantly agreed. Diana tried to get out of it, but Daddy wouldn't let her.

I offered to go first. I hadn't heard Diana practicing all week. I managed to get through my Elizabeth Barrett Browning poem with only a couple of stumbles. Daddy and Lynn applauded as I sat down. Diana looked defeated.

"All right, Diana, your turn," Daddy said.

Diana got up and looked at the floor, and took a deep breath. "I don't know mine yet," she said, "so I'll just read it this time." She opened her book and read:

> Tyger! Tyger! Burning bright
> In the forests of the night,
> What immortal hand or eye
> Could frame thy fearful symmetry?
>
> In what distant deeps or skies
> Burnt the fire of thine eyes
> On what wings dare he aspire?
> What the hand dare seize the fire?
>
> And what shoulder, and what art,
> Could twist the sinews of thy heart?

And when thy heart began to beat,
What dread hand? And what dread feet?

What the hammer? What the chain?
In what furnace was thy brain?
What the anvil? What dread grasp
Dare its deadly terrors clasp?

When the stars threw down their spears,
And watered heaven with their tears,
Did he smile his work to see?
Did he who made the Lamb make thee?

Tyger! Tyger! Burning bright
In the forests of the night,
What immortal hand or eye
Dare frame thy fearful symmetry?

Diana put down the book.

"Well, the first stanza and the last stanza are almost exactly the same, so that will make memorizing easier," Daddy commented.

"One word is different," Diana said. "The word 'could' is changed to 'dare.'"

"Maybe it will help if we talked about the poet and what the poem means."

"I looked up William Blake," Diana said. "He lived over a hundred years ago in England, and he was an engraver. He used to engrave his poems by hand with his own illustrations. See, I printed out a picture of the poem the way he wrote it himself, with a drawing of a tiger. It seems to me like the poem is asking why God would make a creature as fearful as a tiger."

"Do you think the poem says the tiger is evil?" Daddy said.

"Maybe ..." She paused for a moment as if in thought. "Just because a tiger has to kill to eat doesn't make it evil," said Diana. "That's nature. Like, just because the wild stallions fight, that doesn't mean they're evil. Even though I felt the situation was terrible for Firecracker, that's just the way life is in the wild. If you understand the way the stallions feel about the herd, then you understand why they fight. It's just part of nature."

"Right. Wild animals aren't evil," I said. "They're powerful, or fearful."

"Maybe the tiger stands for nature!" said Diana. She had an expression of discovery on her face.

"A metaphor for nature," Daddy said, nodding. "That sounds good."

"Like, think about the storm we had the other night," I said. "The winds and the waves that came all the way up on the dunes, and the trees that fell down. But then the next day the ocean was calm, and the sky was bright blue, and the sun was shining all day. Like, nature is so powerful, and so beautiful!" I said.

"I really like that," Daddy said.

"I picked this poem because I like wild animals," Diana said. "At first I thought it meant, why would God create something like a tiger that is evil? And I didn't like that, because I don't think of any animal as evil."

"Well, one thing to remember," Lynn said, "is that Blake was writing his poem several hundred years ago, and maybe people didn't understand the natural world as well as we do now. Maybe Blake thought tigers were evil."

"And I don't believe in God. And one reason I don't is because there is so much evil," Diana added.

There was a silent moment, and I held my breath. What would Daddy and Lynn say?

Finally Daddy said, "One of the wonderful things about poems is that we read them year after year, and as we get older and wiser, we still get profound meaning from them. You will memorize this poem, and it has a meaning to you now. Ten years from now, you will still remember the poem, but what it means to you by then may be completely different. That's the amazing thing about great literature."

And that was all anyone said. For whatever reason, the moment passed by peacefully. Diana looked at Daddy and nodded. I wondered if Daddy was hoping that maybe in ten years Diana would believe in God. She'd already changed her mind about it once this week. So it was possible.

"Why is tiger spelled with a *y*?" Lynn asked at last.

"It says online that was a common way of spelling tiger back then," Diana said.

"Good choice. Maybe you can practice the poem in the car on the way home," said Lynn.

Later, Diana and Lynn were upstairs together, and Daddy and I were alone downstairs. I knew that this was my chance. I had to do it.

I thought about the things Diana had told me about the horses, about the way their main goal was to keep the herd together. That there was nothing that a young horse wanted more than to be a part of a herd. We had told Daddy and Lynn about Firecracker finding a new herd. I wished my herd—Mama and Daddy and me—could still be together, and sometimes it seemed like a wound that would never heal.

And so now, where was my herd? I wanted to live with Daddy and Lynn, and I had to go through with asking, no matter how much I might hurt Mama's feelings. I had to do what I thought was right, and be where I thought I belonged.

Daddy was bent over the folded newspaper in his lap, but I could see that with one ear he was listening for raised voices upstairs, because Diana was upset about Cody, and she often got upset when she was talking about her dad. I was listening for that too. So far the voices were even and quiet, reasonable, which was amazing. I had never expected things to go well today with her dad, but somehow they had.

I went over and sat on the couch next to Daddy.

"Daddy?" I said.

He looked up from the newspaper, but I could see he wasn't completely focused on me. "Yes, honey?"

"I have something I've been thinking about for a while, but I've been afraid to say anything, because I thought I'd hurt Mama's feelings."

Daddy's expression changed right away. He put the paper aside. "What's that?"

"Well … I was thinking that I'd like to live with you and Lynn."

Daddy's eyes widened, and he bit his lip. "You would?"

"Yeah." I realized I was twirling a piece of my hair and pushed it behind my shoulder and sat on both hands.

"Wow, honey. What's made you decide this?"

"Well, I guess some of it started not too long after

Mama met Barry. I mean, I really wanted her to marry him because I thought we'd be happier, and I loved the wedding and everything. But now I kind of feel left out, and you and Lynn don't make me feel left out."

"We love having you as part of our family, and we want you to be with us whenever you can."

"Also, I just don't think Mama and Barry know what's going on with Matt since he got kicked out of school." I took a breath and plunged ahead. "Matt and his friends stole beer from someone's garage and got drunk one night when Mama and Barry were out."

Daddy's mouth fell open. "Were you there when they were drinking?"

I shook my head. "No, I had spent the night at Casey's house."

"How did you know about it?"

"He bragged about it to me. I've seen him and his friends drinking before, and he threatened to hurt me if I ever told."

Daddy put his chin in his palm, thoughtfully. "Did you say anything to your mother about this, honey?"

My lips felt like they were going to crumple, but I kept them stiff. "I don't want to hurt her feelings."

Daddy suddenly leaned over and pulled me close. "It's okay, you can talk about it," he said. He felt as warm as a bear.

"I know she loves me," I said into his chest. "And I love her so much. I'm afraid she'll get mad at me." It felt like such a relief to say the words. I had been holding them in for so long, because I had thought it would be wimpy to bring it up, and I didn't want to hurt Mama. Even though Daddy didn't make Mama happy when they were married, and she was the one who first wanted the divorce, Daddy ended up hurting Mama's feelings when he married Lynn a few months before Mama married Barry. I didn't want to hurt her again. "Listen, I'm glad you've told me this. Lynn and I would love to have you with us, with all our hearts, and we'll work this out," Daddy said, squeezing my shoulder. "Think about it for a while, and make sure this is really what you want."

"I have been thinking about it for a long time."

Daddy sat quietly for several minutes. Then he asked, "Do you think you can tell your mom this yourself? Or would you like me to say something to her?"

"I know I need to be the one to tell her," I said, sitting up straight and wiping my cheeks. "I can do it."

"It would mean the most coming from you. You could write a letter if that's easier," Daddy said.

"Okay, maybe I will do that," I said. I sat there with him hugging me, and I thought maybe he was crying too, but I didn't look.

23

DIANA

Our car was packed. After Stephanie and I helped Norm attach our bikes to the bike rack on the back of the car, we climbed into the backseat.

"Bye, little house with the triangular window," Lynn said from the passenger seat. "Didn't we have a wonderful time, girls?"

"Yeah," Stephanie said.

I scanned the dunes, looking for one last glimpse of the horses. Leaving a place could be hard sometimes.

"Look," Stephanie said. "Cody's out on his front porch."

I didn't want to look.

"Daddy, can I take a minute to say good-bye to Cody?" she asked.

"That would be nice," Norm said.

She jumped out of the car and ran across the sand, up past the red Mongoose in the yard. I watched her stand there talking with him, smiling and gesturing with her phone, I guess talking about the fact that maybe they'd text each other. His expression was serious, and he only smiled once, when she said her last good-bye. She ran back to the car, and I quickly looked away.

"How can you act like he's still our friend?" I asked.

Stephanie looked at me with a level gaze. "What he did was no worse than what we did last summer with the wolves. He accidentally did something wrong, and he tried not to admit to it. He didn't hurt Isabel on purpose. Remember how last summer you wished Russell would forgive you for what we did? Cody probably feels the same way."

I glanced over at Cody. Stephanie had found out that Cody had to pay a fine, but since he had reported the accident himself, he wasn't charged with a misdemeanor.

On the day after I found out that Cody was the one who hit Isabel, I had gone up to him in the driveway and yelled at him.

"How could you have sat there with me, watching the horse suffer, and known all along that you were the one who did it? How could you have walked around the aquarium with us, knowing that?" I was so mad I was shaking all over. What I couldn't put into words was how betrayed I felt. I had started out not liking him; then I'd changed my mind. And then this!

"I'm sorry. It was an accident," he had said. "I feel terrible."

But I had walked away from him.

Now Mom and Norm waved at Cody as we pulled out of the cul-de-sac. I thought about what Stephanie had said and realized I only had a few more seconds to make up my mind. I lifted my hand and waved.

Without smiling, he pushed his glasses up on his nose and then waved back.

Thirty minutes later we pulled up at a barn, and I jumped out of the car. Mom and Norm had agreed to bring us by to see Dark Angel and Isabel on our way home. I saw Sally's white SUV parked beside the barn. I couldn't wait to see how the horses were doing. "Are they okay?" I yelled to Sally as I crossed the lot.

Sally, standing just outside the barn, looked up and held her finger to her mouth. "Shh!" She rubbed her eyes and looked at me. "The foal is hanging in there."

"Can I see her? Can I help with her?"

I realized that Stephanie had come up behind me. "Can we see her?"

Sally nodded soberly and gestured for us to follow her into the barn. A cone of sunlight cut across the doorway, illuminating floating dust particles. Inside I heard a whinny, and the rich smells of horses and leather and straw relaxed me. This barn was a lot like the one where I rode at home, but bigger. And cleaner. We followed Sally down the central aisle to the first stall on the left. We looked over the half door, and there, lying on a blanket, with her little round feet tucked under her, was the black foal with the blaze on her face. Her mother stood in the stall with her, with a bandaged hind quarter.

I caught my breath. An unexpected, unexplainable feeling of pure love came over me.

"Mom was lucky'" Sally said. "It wasn't broken, only cut and bruised. She'll recover in time. She is starting to walk more. And Dark Angel is nursing regularly."

I looked into Dark Angel's eyes, feathered with dark lashes. I wanted so badly to hold her, to stroke her neck. She scrambled to her feet, standing with locked knees, watching us warily, and then she stepped closer to her mother.

"She's pretty scared," Sally said. "It's to be expected."

While Stephanie and I watched, the foal sidled behind to her mother, then raised her head and began to nurse for a minute or so. Protectively, the mare nuzzled her foal.

"How often does she nurse?" I asked Sally.

"Several times an hour," she said. "She is doing well, and the mother and foal bond is strong, even after the accident. Oh, by the way, I heard from Sergeant Stone that the young man who hit the mare called and confessed."

"Yeah," Stephanie said.

"I heard the rider felt very guilty. He wasn't supposed to be out riding at that time of the night, obviously."

"He was a friend of ours. He felt bad about injuring the mare, and he didn't want to admit that it happened," Stephanie said.

We stood and watched Dark Angel and her mother. I was so, so happy that they were going to be okay. I wanted to tell Dad about her. When we got home, I'd call and tell him all about it. I thought of flying up in the sky with him, seeing all around us, and the way he suddenly seemed to pay attention to me.

"Everything is going to be okay," I told Stephanie. "Everything is going to be okay."

Mom came in with Norm and took out the camera, and Sally let us go into the stall so she could snap a picture of us with Dark Angel. We leaned our heads down next to the foal's so we could be cheek to cheek when the shutter clicked.

Sally came back and stood with Mom and Norm outside the stall door.

"How long before Dark Angel and her mother can go back to the herd?" Stephanie asked.

The foal seemed relaxed and leaned the weight of her little body against her mother.

"You know that she can never go back to the herd," Sally said.

"Oh no!" Stephanie said. "Why not?"

I knew but let Sally answer.

"Because she will be tamed and friendly toward humans by then. She will be used to depending on us for food, and that's not a good thing for the wild herd."

"What will happen to her?" Mom asked.

"She will be adopted out," Sally said. "There are lots of potential owners out there who would love to have a pretty little Spanish mustang like Dark Angel. Don't worry. We'll make sure she has a loving home."

Oh, what if we could adopt Dark Angel? Would it be possible? That would be the most amazing thing. I felt like I'd never wanted anything so much as that.

"Oh, Mom! Can we adopt her?" I said. Deep inside I knew the answer, because we didn't have a barn, but I just had to ask anyway.

Mom smiled. "I wish I could say yes! But you know we don't have anywhere to keep a horse. I'm sure they will keep you posted on how she's doing."

Mom and Sally moved away, talking. Stephanie and I stayed and kept watching the foal. So she could never go back to the herd. And that was the way of nature. Nature, as the poet William Blake had written, was a fearsome thing.

"Stephanie," I said, "People talk about me at school."

She looked at me with surprise. "I didn't know you knew."

"Yeah. They call me 'Animal.'"

Stephanie was silent for a long time, and then she said, "I've felt bad because I haven't stood up for you. I'm sorry about that. I feel so bad."

"You shouldn't," I said, shaking my head. "I have to stand up for myself. In a way, you standing up for me could make things worse for both of us."

Stephanie thought about that. "Well, you could take being called 'animal' as a compliment. I mean, look how tough animals are."

"I do," I said. I thought about how I'd gotten so much closer to Stephanie on this vacation and how I was able

261

to talk to her heart to heart. I felt like I could really trust her.

"Got to get on the road, girls," Norm called from the barn entrance. With last good-byes to Dark Angel and her mother, we headed back to the car, blinking in the bright sunlight after the darkness of the barn. Sally stood at the barn entrance to say good-bye.

"Thanks! Can I write you to see how they're doing?" I said.

"Sure. My pleasure," Sally said. She disappeared again into the barn.

An hour later, we had just crossed the second bridge and were driving along a straight stretch of highway with marshland on both sides. I was feeling depressed about having to go back to school next week, when traffic slowed and several cars backed up in front of us. We craned our necks to look out the window and saw about three cars parked beside the road, and people standing on the shoulder, some with binoculars and others with cameras. They were all staring at something in the black water.

"Wonder what's going on?" Mom said.

We inched closer, staring at the spot where the people's attention was directed.

"I see it!" Stephanie said.

And then I saw too. Two yellow eyes and two small nostrils, motionless, just on the surface of the water.

"An alligator!" I said. And I thought again of the William Blake poem. Nature was fearsome. Every animal preyed on another. Everywhere in nature there were predators, both seen and unseen. The horses couldn't survive without the herd. In the maritime forest, the twisted trees needed each other for protection from the winds and salt spray. For all living things, life was hard, and living things needed each other.

But I was here with my family, Mom and Norm and Stephanie too. Our car moved onto the last bridge for the mainland, and we headed out over the long, low span over the Alligator River.

"Hey, Steph," I said. "Will you help me practice my poem?"

"Sure," she said. "I'm happy to help."

The End

ACKNOWLEDGMENTS

I'd like to thank the following people for their help with this book:

Karen McAlpin and Wesley Stallings from the Wild Horse Fund for giving me background on the Corolla wild horses;

Lee Lofland for his knowledge of police procedure;

Kevin Ward, the youth director of Williamson's Chapel Methodist Church for allowing me to visit the youth group;

The youth groups of Williamson's Chapel Methodist Church and North Cross Church for welcoming me and being so open about their feelings and opinions;

Ann Campanella and her daughter, Sydney, for reading and commenting;

Chris Woodworth for her invaluable help with plot questions;

Dan and Betsy Clark for introducing us to the Outer Banks back before our children were even born;

And last but not least, Deb Waldron for patiently listening to my character and plot permutations on a daily basis.

Talk It Up!

Want free books?
First looks at the best new fiction?
Awesome exclusive merchandise?

We want to hear from you!

Give us your opinions on titles, covers, and stories.
Join the Z Street Team.

Email us at zstreetteam@zondervan.com
to sign up today!

Also—Friend us on Facebook!

www.facebook.com/goodteenreads

- Video Trailers
- Connect with your favorite authors
- Sneak peeks at new releases
- Giveaways
- Fun discussions
- And much more!